Woman EX

The human race is about to change.

by Réal Laplaine

Cover design by Cindy Anderson

First edition published 9 March 2018
Second edition published 9 October 2019

Books by Réal Laplaine

Intrusion: A Keeno Crime Thriller (Book I)
Quantum Assault: A Keeno Crime Thriller (Book II)
The One: A Keeno Crime Thriller (Book III)
The 9th Divinity: A Keeno Crime Thriller (Book IV)
Earth Escape: The Ultimate Space Odyssey
Twilight Visitor: It takes only 8 minutes to set the world on fire.
Deception People: Telling the truth can be fatal.
The Other: Her past life won't let go.
The Buffalo Kid: A second chance at life turns into a bizarre thriller.
Dead but not Gone: Hollywood's iconic blonde returns from the grave.
Finding Agnetha: A dream to reunite ABBA sparks a global event.
Woman EX: Women have taken over a broken world.
When Gods Roar: The Awakening
See Me Not: A story about undying hope.
When Cowboys Fall
V.O.I.C.E. – The Silence is Over!

For more information about the author go to www.reallaplaine.com

“…their time is up!”

Oprah Winfrey

“Science gives us power, a power that must be in balance with our humanity if we are to advance as people and as a culture.”

Anonymous

Dedicated to the new generation.

Some facts to consider…

While Woman EX is a work of fiction, there are certain facts and truths which form the weave of this story:

- There exist 15,000 (or more) documented nuclear warheads in arsenals, 90% of which are in the hands of the United States of America and Russia. These bombs are many times more powerful than the atomic bombs dropped on Japan at the end of World War II.
- Studies show that roughly 10% of the world's nations, as of this writing, are headed by women, and none of those nations possess weapons of mass destruction, nor are they major players in the global military arena.
- The Taurids is a meteor shower that happens annually, originating from a comet called Encke. The meteor shower is the result of pieces of that comet breaking off and burning up in our atmosphere as Encke passes by.
- Astrophysicists have been warning us about the potential of large rocks someday coming our way. It is theorized that the Ice Age was the result of just one large meteor striking the Earth and enveloping it with so much dirt and particulates that it literally blocked the sun's

warming rays and plummeted temperatures to freezing.

- Krakatoa, the volcanic eruption which occurred in 1883 in the archipelago of what is now known as Indonesia, is still considered the most powerful natural explosion in known history. It resulted in climatic changes and darkened the skies around the globe for upwards of five years.
- Hundreds of reputable engineers, scientists and demolition experts around the world have provided creditable material showing that the incident known as 9/11, when two planes struck the twin towers in New York City on the 11th of September 2001, could not possibly have destroyed those towers as the US government claimed. Additionally, the 3rd building which fell that same day, known as *building 7*, a forty-seven-story structure across the street, was never even hit by anything, and yet, it too crumbled to the ground in perfect-demolition-style – an incidental occurrence which was generally accepted without question because US officials claimed it too was the victim of the attack.

The Tree of Life

The tree had withstood the test of time. In fact, even before time was measured, the tree was already a strapping youngster, that is, as far as trees go.

The world had circumvented the sun more times than could be counted, during which, the seedling had become a towering and mature adult, and it measured that passing time by the rings which formed around the girth of its broad trunk.

It was a proud and dignified tree, and every day that the sun rose was a joyful day in the knowledge that it provided life to the forest all around it; and by night, security and protection, warmth and cover to the creatures who lived beneath and within it.

It stood strong, bearing its leaves, and providing nourishment and life-giving oxygen to the world around, while its roots provided the means of existence for creatures beneath the soil.

As it lifted its leaves to the rising sun, the air was thick with a wondrous scent – the smell of the most tantalizing bouquet of all – life itself!

A small shudder trembled within its boughs, a joyful quiver that quaked to its living soul and reached out to the very tips of its leaves which now twisted upwards to embrace the life-giving rays of morning light.

A bird landed and perched on one of its great arms. Its head rocked back and forth in search of something to eat. It was a ritual that Tree loved.

Suddenly the bird froze.

What could it be, thought Tree?

The forest seemed calm enough, the air was gentle – nothing was out of place; but as Tree listened, it sensed it too; a disquieting feeling, a strange dissonance in the taciturnity.

An unsettling trembling soon touched its roots, a tangible vibration passed along through the network that trees used to talk with one another.

The trembling grew and waxed, rattling the forest.

Suddenly the sky lit up with a brilliant and explosive light, hot and scorching, it screeched outward like a million bursting suns, sending a shuddering and ground-breaking thunderous shockwave that shook Tree to its very core.

Seconds later, the air burned incandescent, and Tree watched in horror as its leaves turned from brilliant green to deathly withered black, as its countless life-giving tendrils and arms were scorched beyond recognition, and as its very bark began to blister and bubble under the assault of the living flames that consumed it.

The roar of a raging wind bent the stout tree, threatening to pull it from the ground, the place it had stood for generations; and only by the force of sheer will to survive did it hold onto life.

As it shouldered the horrendous attack, it watched as the forest around it was blighted beyond recognition, as companion trees who had stood their ground as long, or longer, were shredded and burned to lifeless stalks of black.

When the storm passed, the scent of death was everywhere, and a black acrid smoke choked the very air.

In the distance, a massive cloud mushroomed upward, pressing into the heavens, like a beastly horror from another world.

Tree sighed as apathy replaced vibrant life, and slowly, irrevocably, it slumped and soon died in silent agony.

-I-

1

The mood was high amongst the crew of *Dauntless.*

It had been over sixteen years since they left Earth on a trip that spanned millions of kilometers to reach Europa and then back again.

Just one of sixty-six planetoids which orbited Jupiter, Europa had been their base for almost three of those years, while the rest of the time was spent in Hyper-Sleep-Stasis, or HSS, that is, six years there and six years back inside sleep-pods.

Had it not been for the launch of the *Hubble2 Deep Space Telescope,* and the *James Webb Space Telescope,* the Jupiter Mission would not have come into existence.

They changed everything, providing ground-breaking and breathtaking images and spectral scans showing that there was water beneath the icy plains of Europa, which meant a high probability of finding life under its frozen wasteland.

While Mars missions were already eagerly being pursued, and corporations were lining up like soldiers outside a brothel in the hopes of being the first to harvest the red planet's resources, others saw Europa as having far more profound implications for the future of our race. In fact, with geopolitical events escalating as they were, and the continued threats of nuclear assaults bouncing like ping-pong balls between America, North Korea and Russia, NASA regarded Europa as a critical step toward its dream of colonizing one of several exoplanets which had been found over recent years and which showed signs of being habitable.

No one really considered Europa a candidate for mass-colonization, but those involved in the project did see it as a high probability in providing answers to the question – *is there life out there*, and if so, *what is it?* And with that question answered, it could serve as a springboard to launching humankind to the distant stars.

While stupid men played Russian roulette with the future of humanity, brighter minds at NASA and ESA, the European Space Agency, were racing against the clock.

The *Dauntless,* the largest spacecraft ever conceived, was designed, assembled, and put into orbit around Earth in record time – the direct result of the collective effort of many nations. NASA was elected to oversee the mission, but the matrix of the Jupiter Mission was a collaborative one.

The ship measured the length of three large school buses placed end-to-end.

The HAB, the unit its crew would live in while on Europa's surface, was a detachable appendage to the lower hull of the *Dauntless*. And while the ship was often humorously referred to as the Dill because of its shape which resembled a pickle, the HAB was entirely devoid of any aesthetic qualities whatsoever, appearing more like a shipping container, with squared features, and having minimalistic navigational acuity required to land it on Europa, and then take off again where it would couple with the *Dauntless* which would remain in orbit high above.

It was a bold move, but those behind the program went ahead with the mission despite the groans of an American leadership more interested in military parades, Twitter *likes* and sterilizing and protecting America from the undocumented immigrants "infiltrating" it – in fact, much of the funding came through ESA's pipeline, not America's.

Tanner McNeal, its captain, sat quietly watching the Visio - a holographic display of their trajectory back to Earth, as a toothpick idly floated between his lips.

He could hardly believe his eyes – Earth was now in view of the ship's telemetry – not just a digital schematic, but an actual pinprick of light, one that was now perceptible in the sea of countless white dots on the screen ahead.

When they had set off on the mission, he and his crew had been younger men and women – most of them in their mid-twenties – himself being the oldest, having just turned twenty-nine the day after the launch.

After coupling with the *Dauntless*, which had been put into orbit months before and was already stocked and ready for their journey, three women and seven men, himself included, went into Sub-Sleep-Stasis two weeks into the voyage. It was a necessary, but dreaded and terrifying aspect of the mission, because for six years they laid in a slimy goop, one which keep their bodies at just the right temperature, while a cocktail of sedatives slowed their physiological processes down to an induced state of comatose, as close to death as sustainably possible. It was a shadow-dance with the Grim Reaper, who stood toe-to-toe on the other side of a very thin line, while a tenuous life-support system provided their sedated bodies with a protein based-saline solution fed directly into their veins, keeping them fed and hydrated.

Now, so close to finishing their mission, the longest ever endeavored by any star navigator, Tanner afforded himself the luxury of daydreaming, unleashing his mind from the rigors required of him as captain.

There was still a major hurdle ahead of them, he knew that, but it felt good to let the mental steam bleed off.

A boisterous laugh emitted from behind him, yanking Tanner from his mental maundering.

“I wonder,” began Camilla, a native Venezuelan who specialized in microbiology and bioengineering, and was also known for her skills as an

IT-guru, cyber pirate, and master computer hacker, "if our years away from Earth will categorize us as cosmic dummies?"

Petar, the ship's geologist and mineral expert, an out-spoken Serbian who often said exactly what was on his mind without concern for the consequences, responded. "You mean we're going look culturally retarded to everyone back home – is that it?"

"Not retarded, but certainly uninformed."

"Ahh," Petar raised a brow, "like Robinson Crusoe coming back to civilization after being stuck on an island?"

Camilla shrugged. "Look how fast technology changed between the Millennium and when we fired off to Jupiter. In the last sixteen years since we have been gone, it could have advanced exponentially, we do not know, especially since we have had no communication with Earth for most of our mission."

Rose, a Brit, the ship's physicist, and quantum specialist, known for being confrontational at any opportunity, chimed into the discussion. "Oh, you mean the fact that the very last transmission we received was that some ass-fuck in North Korea was threatening to start World War III?" She said with a sneer and a raised brow.

Camilla, being a consummate optimist and diametrically opposed to Roses' disposition, shrugged.

"We really don't know if that happened."

Rose cast her another look of challenge. “And, what if it did? What if that is the reason for the com-blackout?”

For a long moment, the crew went silent as the haunting visions filled the void, the informational abyss that followed whenever the subject of the com-blackout was broached.

Matis, a Lithuanian and the ship’s engineering and electronics specialist, not to mention the *fix-it-all-guy*, entered the dialogue now. “Let us not dither on the negative, ladies. I prefer to think that they finally mastered cyber-dolls,” he smiled with a mock leer and a playful flick of his brow.

Michael Brenner, the native Texan, ship’s horticulturist and cook, raised a finger to the air as if on cue. “That would be cool.”

“Oh, for god’s sake!” exclaimed Rose. “Get your fook’n hormones under control guys. That’s disgusting!” she announced with an affected look of repulsion, accented by her Welsh dialect.

Brenner waved her off with a flick of his hand.

“You’re just jealous.”

“Of you?!” She cackled. “If you want to have sex with dolls, be my guest. I prefer the real thing.”

Tanner cracked a smile. The banter was good. It would help them deal with the mental challenges they would all soon face.

The big question that had plagued them during the entire mission, since the day they had awoken from

HSS as they neared Europa, was why the connection with NASA, for that matter, Earth, had ceased. It was an impossible question to answer, because without that link, it was all guesswork.

Compounding that issue was the fact that NASA psychologists had warned him that his crew would very likely have to endure SDD, *Severe-Discontinuity-Disorder,* a member of the *Post-Trauma-Stress-Disorder* family of mental conditions that had first been diagnosed in veterans of war, who, upon returning home, found themselves besieged by the horrors of war, and feeling disenfranchised from the society they had left.

Telanthia, usually referred to as Tel by most, sidled next to where Tanner sat.

Her sudden appearance caused his heart to skip a beat.

"I have been meaning to ask you a question."

Tanner looked up at her perfect face. The Icelandic native, with silver-white hair cascading to her shoulders, like icy water pitching from a glacier, and those azure eyes and skin a hue of cream, smiled down at him.

As always, Tanner felt as if she was a goddess who had crash-landed on Earth. Since first seeing her, back at Johnson Space Center, that face, those eyes, the entire package, still had the same effect on him.

“Why the toothpicks, Tanner?” she asked, her head lightly bobbing as her eyes followed the sliver of wood precariously perched on his lower lip.

“Why not?”

“Because we’re eating puree and powdered food, it’s not as if you need to pick your teeth after a steak dinner.”

Tanner grinned. “Call it a coping-mechanism.”

“Interesting. Seems to me like you have a toothpick fetish,” she said with a playful grin and flick of her brow.

“Sure, put a Freudian spin on it if you like.”

She reciprocated with her usual Mona Lisa-like smile – both beautiful and alluring somehow.

“Captain,” the voice rocked Tanner from his light flirtation. He turned to Mav, his 1st Officer, who had a look of deep concern rippling across his face. Mav tipped his head at the console.

The discussions in the control room suddenly ceased as the undercurrent of apprehensive anxiety which had kept a constant grip on the crew since coming out of HSS, now caused them all to turn and look at the holographic display.

“What the hell is that?” asked Tanner as he leaned forward and peered at the strange code streaming across the screen.

Mav shrugged. “Looks like Earth is finally talking to us, Cap.”

2

"Mission Control, this is captain Tanner McNeal of the *Dauntless*."

The line remained deathly silent - again.

Frustrated, he turned to Matis. "You're absolutely sure the ship's com-link is intact?"

"I tested it five times, Cap," answered the man. "I even bounced signals off a Sat-dish on the moon, and each time, our telemetry picked up the return signal without error." He paused to nod toward the screen. "The problem is Earth-side. They are not answering us."

"I just don't get it," said Tanner, his frustration mounting. "First, we get this strange code, but then no one answers."

Mav leaned back, crossing his arms with a grin fixed to his lips. "Maybe aliens finally took over."

"That would be an upgrade," announced Rose, who listened in nearby.

Tanner sighed. Seventeen years ago, during their final training sessions at NASA, they had been briefed on all the possible contingencies, a mental safety-net to prepare them for the fact that the planet they returned to might not be the same place they had left. The mad escalation of nuclear weapons at the time they lifted off for Jupiter, the mushrooming military forces assembled along borders between East and

West, the global-warming, et al, all of it was a sign that if a madman started the domino-effect, it could very well end with Earth spiraling back into a regressive state.

Sobering as the briefings had been, none of the crew, himself included, really considered that anyone would let things go that far south – but ever since the com-blackout early in their mission, that mindset had changed – and now, this radio silence was inviting the worst possible visions to infiltrate his mind.

Tanner swiveled his chair to face the rest of his crew. A cocktail of pent-up emotions was clearly etched on their faces; like roads crisscrossing a landscape, the full gamut, including excitement, worry, doubt, dread, anticipation, fear, a force that pounded inside each of them, like waves smashing into a beach.

Tanner had pondered over this day, hoping it would never come, hoping that somehow, NASA would re-establish contact with them – but that day never arrived – and the absence of communication for years now, piqued a cognizant sense that whatever was happening back on Earth, it was not good.

"We have to assume the worst-case scenario at this point," said Tanner to the rest of the crew.

"And what is your take on the worst?" asked Deptha, the Indian and geological specialist from Mumbai, the seventh member of the male crew.

Tanner shrugged. "I don't know, Dep, use your imagination."

“I assume,” began Telanthia, taking the opportunity to exert her role as the group’s behavioral specialist and matron, “that we are invoking contingencies for the possibility of a hostile reception?”

“Definitely,” responded Tanner. “I have activated *Mandate 666.* The ship’s computer is locked to any outside access. If things go sideways, it will be hard for anyone to access our research records or the ship’s log without at least two of us entering the passcode.”

Petar shook his head, a look of vacant confusion painted on his face. “What about *Footprint*?”

All faces turned to Tanner. “Until we know what the scene is on Earth, *Footprint* remains a secret.”

3

Like brittle ice on the verge of shattering, tensions were at an apex as the *Dauntless* swept into orbit around Earth.

The entire crew stared in utter silence as the African continent, framed between an azure ocean of water on all sides, slid by.

The Sahara, the grand master of deserts, in all its primordial beauty, capped the continent like tawny leather; and within seconds, the Nile, its gaping mouth fanning out into the Mediterranean, broke the tarnish of endless desert with a wash of lush and fertile green that merged into the waiting arms of the Mediterranean. It was a mesmerizing sight, during which not a word was spoken.

They had not seen Earth for over sixteen years, and though no one ever showed it, or said it, it is doubtless that each of them wondered at some time during their mission if they ever would. But now, as they looked down on this one in a billion beauty in the fold of the cosmic expanse, it haunted them with specters of a cataclysm – was it war, or disease – why was Earth not talking to them?

What could explain this hellish silence echoing up from a world of billions of people?

Tanner was now reminded of a duty incumbent on him as the captain, one that he was not looking forward to doing. He would have to contact Brett Pearson's family once they landed. The New Zealander and ship's astrophysicist, had been their only casualty, reminding him, that despite her allure, the enchanter, space, was a merciless bitch when it came to compliance to her terms of engagement. Brett had turned his back on her, an incautiousness moment when he tripped and fell into a cavity during one of their excursions into the unknown realm of Europa. A jagged edge of a protruding rock tore his suit, exposing him to the icy grip of space, and before anyone could get to him, she had sucked the life from him, leaving a frozen cadaver in its place.

Tanner was no stranger to death. As a test-pilot in the Netherlands, before joining up with the European Space Agency, he had attended more than one funeral of men who had crashed their planes. And while he did not fear death, the frozen eyes of Brett Pearson staring up at him through his visor on that day, reminded him that death's grip was irrevocable – you could not turn back the clock on it.

He turned to Mav, who sat next to him at the ship's console.

"You still hailing NASA?"

"Yup! She ain't sing'n yet, Cap," answered Mav with a playful lilt. "What do you want to do?"

Tanner thought for a time before answering.

"Fuck it, take her down."

Mav confirmed the coordinates one last time, ensuring that their glide-path was precise. If they came in too acutely, the friction could burn through the ship's protective shielding and kill them all. Come in too low and they would bounce off the atmosphere, careening back into space, and with all the space-junk and abandoned satellites floating in that graveyard around the planet, it opened the door for a fender-bender, or worse.

Mav manually nosed the *Dauntless* downward, touching the outmost layer of the atmosphere. With no beacon coming from NASA, it was unlikely that the ship's autopilot would function as it should. Nonetheless, as with every other NASA pilot before him, he had been trained for just such a manual re-entry.

"Hold onto your privates," he announced with a wide grin as he rolled the ship to the left and then gently eased the Dauntless on a steeper angle. Within seconds, the roller-coaster ride began. The front of the ship lit up as the friction between metal and air sparked a brilliant display of yellow, orange, and red – as if someone had a blowtorch to its nose.

The G-force accelerated rapidly, crushing them into their seats with more gravitational force than they had experienced since taking off from Earth years before. Muffled groans escaped their lips as their chests and ribs felt the pressure, evoking even more muted sounds of pain.

The ship began to rock, like a kite in a blistering wind, as the forward portion now glowed as bright as the crimson of red-hot iron being heated to molten metal.

"*Now entering lower atmosphere*," announced the computer. "*ETA three minutes and three seconds*."

As the *Dauntless* broke through the final layer, sounds of relief followed as the pressure eased. Mav lowered the speed, skillfully navigating the ship into a sweeping and graceful turn, arcing it out over the coastline. The waters of the Pacific Ocean gleamed and greeted them. It was a sight that caused a sense of awe to pervade the crew.

"*Approaching final glide path,*" said the computer as Mav incrementally brought the ship in line with the stretch of runway ahead, a mere sliver in the high desert that bordered the Mojave beyond.

"Landing gear down," commanded Mav to the computer. The holographic projection showed the wheels lowering and locking into position, the first time they had been activated in over sixteen years.

Everyone sighed with relief.

The terrain swept by, just a blur of shapes and colors, as the *Dauntless* kissed the asphalt with the tenderness of a lover's touch. "*Chutes deployed,*" announced the computer, and with that, the ship lurched backwards, as if a giant had suddenly clutched it in the palm of its hand. It slowed from its landing speed of over 550 kilometers and within seconds, it coasted to a stop.

"*Welcome home*," flashed the words on the panel ahead.

Tanner rolled his eyes at the irony of the statement. *Home?!*

He unbuckled, stood, and suddenly felt a strange sensation, one he had not experienced for over one and a half decades - Earth's gravity.

Taking a cautious step – he teetered, like a baby taking its first steps. He had to remind himself that after so long in either zero-G of space or the reduced gravity of Europa, that his muscles had atrophied; and despite the exercise regimens they had done in preparation for this moment, their bodies would still have to endure a re-acclimation period.

"Everyone okay?" he asked. The question was met by pale looks and faces covered in sweat, testimony to the strain they had just endured – but at the same time, their eyes betrayed their growing excitement.

Telanthia was busily assessing the atmosphere outside. She looked up at Tanner with a curious and dumbfounded look, "I'm not picking up anything unusual."

"Good! Open main hatch," he commanded the computer.

A series of clicks and hisses followed as the thick metal door snapped open with a loud pop, and instantly, the differential between the ship's internal pressure and that of Earth accosted their ears.

Like water rushing into an empty well, the ship's-controlled atmosphere flushed out to meet Earths', while a wave of warm and sultry air flushed inward, filling the ship with the scent of dry desert sage, the acrid taste of dust and sand, the pungent odor of asphalt heated by the burning sun, all of it the very perfume of Earth herself. It was an olfactory overload, like a sudden injection of heroin streaming through their veins and causing a euphoric feeling of ecstasy.

Tanner gingerly poked his head out into the world and squinted. It was the first time he truly felt warmth and the stark glare of a sun, since leaving on the mission. It felt wonderful.

With a quick glance back at the anticipating eyes watching him, he gingerly stepped down the ladder, rung by rung, the muscles in his legs screaming at every step, finally landing on the runway, and feeling, as he had already felt, the firm grip of Earth's gravity pulling him into her embrace.

The rest of the crew did not wait a second longer, and despite their weakened muscles and teetering legs, the sounds of pleasure emitting from them sounded like that of young children excitedly jumping in puddles of water.

Despite the overwhelming relief of being back on Earth, Tanner's sense of wariness was exacerbated by the strange silence. As much as he loved its embrace, in fact, regarding silence as his greatest therapy, this was not the right time for it.

Where was everyone, he thought?

They had just returned from the most daring mission ever embarked upon – certainly, there should be someone to meet them?

Dread began to fill his soul, like water brimming the top of a glass, while the cognitive voice deep inside was telling him that something was very wrong.

As he walked, he focused his eyes on the distant foothills which shimmered and vacillated through a veil of heated air that diffused and played with the light.

Sage brush gently rolled by in the distance, bouncing and careening along the ground like players in a game.

A group of buildings and hangers shimmered on one side of the runway. It all looked much the same as he remembered it to be, but the silence filled him with a dystopian sense of bewilderment.

Mav approached, raising, and lowering his feet like a marionette controlled by a puppeteer. "Wow, this feels so weird,"

In the distance, a flickering phantom caught their eyes. "Looks like we've got company, Cap," said Mav pointing to a cluster that morphed and grew, soon manifesting as a column of vehicles racing toward them at high speed.

Reflexively, Tanner gripped his weapon, slipping the safety off. Mav did the same, as did the rest of the crew, who now gathered around with their hands poised near the guns strapped to their sides.

They watched with anxious eyes as trucks came to a screeching halt in a cloud of dust, and as uniformed figures poured out with their weapons trained on them.

It was as if their worst nightmares were now coming true.

This was not a reception, clearly, it was a confrontation.

With a soldier-like stride, a woman advanced to within a meter of Tanner. “You are Captain Tanner McNeal of the star ship *Dauntless*, correct?” Her words broke the torrid air with a harsh military cadence.

“Yes.”

“And these are your crew?” she tipped her head at the others.

“They are?”

“Then, I must inform you that you and your crew are hereby placed under arrest.”

Tanner felt a wave of shock streaking through him, like a bolt of lightning.

“What?!” He exclaimed. “Arrest, for what?”

“You are hereby prisoners under the *Inhumane Act*.”

“What are you talking about,” he shouted, the angst suddenly funneling up like an exploding oil well, as he stepped toward her.

The woman calmly raised a hand and in a fraction of a second, a literal swarm of objects, no larger than the size of a hand, silently streaked into position directly above Tanner and the others. They hung there menacingly, with their ocular domes emitting a blue neon light which fanned over their faces.

She stepped closer, while the swarm advanced in equal measure, until Tanner was looking into the optic eye of one just above him.

"Resistance is futile, Captain. These drones are equipped with advanced weaponry. You and your crew will be dead in less than three seconds if I command it."

-II-

1

From intrepid space voyageurs and pioneers trespassing into the domain of the gods themselves, to now, a morbid group of prisoners locked inside two cells; the men in one, and the women in an adjacent cell – their amazing journey had come to an outlandish end.

In all their imagination over the years in space, this scenario never played out in the theater of their minds.

This was the ne-plus-ultra of contradictions, the flipside of existential irony. The most significant space mission ever endeavored by humanity, ending in such a way – treated as enemies of the state, was satire at its best.

It was as if they had landed in an episode of the Twilight Zone, where *up was now down*, and *right was now wrong*.

Tanner stood facing a thick glass wall with a covey of guards staring back at him from the other side. Their prison was a glass box – tantamount to being in a fishbowl.

The adjacent cell, holding Telanthia, Rose and Camilla was the same. The glass was so thick that it permitted no sounds to pass between them.

He stole a look at Tel, her ice-blue eyes were filled with the same consternation he felt.

Mav stepped up to where he stood. "What do you think, Cap?" asked Mav as he purposefully glared at a guard who looked back at him as if he did not even exist. Mav provoked her with a wink as he turned to Tanner.

"I have no idea, Mav. But did you notice…?"

"You mean, no men?"

"Yeah. I did not see a single male between here and Edwards Air Force Base."

"Me neither. And where is *here*, anyhow," replied Mav.

Just then, the door at the far end of the corridor swung open. A trio of women marched in with a military-like stride, uniformed in tight black leather pants, black knee-high-boots, and a black vest – not to mention the weapons they carried. The entire package was a throwback, as if they were suddenly reliving a campy science fiction film.

They stopped in front of the cell, and as they did, both Tanner and Mav noticed the logo emblazoned on their vest.

Two of the guards raised their weapons at them as the third touched her wrist to a metal plate and the thick glass wall hushed upward into the ceiling.

"Captain, McNeal, follow me," she commanded with a frosty look on her face.

Tanner stepped from the cell, and as he did, the glass wall slid back into place, separating him from the rest of his crew.

2

Tanner was escorted to a conference room ringed by black leather chairs but without a centerpiece table. At the end of the room sat one golden chair.

A guard pointed with the tip of her weapon – waiting for him to comply and sit.

The entire ordeal was disconcerting to say the least; from the point of landing back on Earth, to being arrested and transported to this place, Tanner's head was awash with a continuous storm of questions.

After what seemed an inordinate amount of time, the door to the room swung open, and in strode a woman. Unlike the guards who wore tight-fitting black leathers, her entire outfit was blood-red – also emblazoned with the same logo on her vest.

Wrapped around her lower right arm and upper hand was a black leather thong, as if demarcating her of special office.

She was unequivocally beautiful, but as he watched her enter, Tanner quickly realized that her beauty alluded to a certain lethality – like an alluring flower with a deadly sting.

It was the nuances of her body language that flagged the warning in his mind. Narrow deep-set eyes probed him. Perfectly manicured nails painted a tint that precisely matched her red leathers and which she carried like lethal weapons, while stark-black hair tapered like stilettos to a precise point on each side of her face. She exuded an unchallengeable air of authority.

As she sat, she cast a fleeting glance his way, as if he were a mere wall fixture.

It was an icy reception, portentous of nothing good.

Finally, she tipped her head to one side with a mildly inquisitive, yet subtle look of disparagement in her eyes, and spoke, "I assume you have many questions, Captain McNeal."

"You assume right."

"You may call me Lady V."

Tanner raised a questioning brow. "Until I know what's going on, I'm not calling you anything."

She grinned, a snake-like gesture. "A rebel to the end, uh?"

"You arrested us – what did you expect?"

She chuckled derisively, obviously amused.

"Nonetheless, you will come to respect me in due time, Tanner." She flicked a hand to the air. "I am the President."

"Of what?"

"New America."

Tanner was confused. "What do you mean, New America?"

A cat-like grin spread across her lips – manifestly clear that she was enjoying exacerbating the confusion which played across Tanner's face like a full orchestra.

"Unfortunately," she began as she stood and walked the room "despite your historic return there will be no applauding masses, no tickertape parades or Presidential pats on the backs for you or your crew."

"I got that idea when we were met with guns in our faces."

"A necessary precaution," she said with a dismissive shrug.

"Why?"

Her eyes twisted up to meet his, "It's not the same world you left nearly seventeen years ago."

"No fucking kidding," he said gruffly. "If you're the President, why are you talking to me?"

"Because Tanner McNeal, you are a member of an endangered species."

3

Tel stared through the wall of their glass prison with her eyes fixed on the distant door – the very one that Tanner had disappeared through.

She sighed, longing to see him again.

Her mind idled back to a time on Europa, when she and Tanner had sat on a rocky knoll overlooking the white expanse of a vast icy plain, one they had dubbed *Wonderland.*

Like all things on Europa, its visceral beauty transcended anything she had ever known back on Earth – even her own country of origin, Iceland. Every way they looked, the universe, an endless ocean of stars, gawked back at them. It was always a transcendent moment, an experience she loved sharing with Tanner, because while they could not be open about the love they felt, being under strict orders from NASA to engage no inter-crew relations for the duration of the mission, it was their moment, a tacit statement of something that they shared between them.

"What do you think is happening back on Earth?" she had asked him one day. She could tell by his hesitant response that her question had sent him to another place. His head bobbed, the icy image of the terrain around them reflected in his visor as he did.

"I'd like to think it's nothing, but my gut says differently."

"I assume it isn't a good feeling?"

"You know I have to put up the best possible face for the rest of the crew – keep morale high and all that shit."

"I know," she answered.

He looked away, immersing his eyes in the sheer awesomeness of Europa's empty domain. "I don't think it's good, Tel. Whatever has happened back on Earth, it's definitely not good – otherwise we would have heard from someone since the blackout."

His words now rang in her head, like the haunting wail of a siren in a fog-ridden sea, warning sailors of approaching rocks. It seemed that Tanner's sense, back then was correct because none of this was good.

Rose, the fair-skinned Welsh member of the crew, with her mantle of thick flaming-red hair girding her face like a lion's mane, shuffled over to where Tel sat.

"Ya know you're gonna burn a hole in that glass if you keep staring at it," she said with a wry smile – her accent, as always, adding spice to any utterance.

Tel sighed, her shoulders sagging slightly with the weight of her thoughts. "I don't understand any of this, do you?" She turned to her with a desperate look in her eyes.

Rose shook her head. "Not a fook'n clue, Lass.

Whatever it is," she tipped her head at the guards outside, "it is weird. I have not seen any men, not during our entire trip here."

"Me neither," uttered Tel, as she glanced at the other members of their crew who sat in the adjacent cell – the very men who were like brothers to her, the most significant and important men in her life.

4

Tanner's world was reeling from the woman's statement.

"I don't understand - what are you talking about?"

Lady V tipped her head at him with a look that was neither sympathetic nor empathetic, more like pity. "Are you a believer of prophecy or karma, Captain?"

"No."

She grinned sardonically, a gesticulation that often dominated her face.

"Maybe this narrative will change your perspective," she said as she tapped a slim metal wrist band, bringing a holographic Visio or HV, into view – its 3D imagery hanging in the air between them with surrealistic realism.

"This is a computer simulation put together in the wake of what we refer to as the *Cataclysm* – an event that happened several months after you rocketed off to Europa."

Tanner watched the digital simulation.

She points to a comet now approaching Earth in the simulation. "That is the Encke, which, as you probably already know from your training, is a regular visitor by our shores and provides us with noteworthy meteor showers…"

"The Taurids, I know," he said without taking his eyes from the Visio.

"Unfortunately, as you will see," she lingered and waited as two large rocks dipped their heads from the trailing channels of the comet, and then, dropped into a direct path with Earth. "Encke not only gave us a meteor show that year, but it also sent us two very special ambassadors."

The impact was startling – as if the Earth would split in half. It was shocking in its magnitude.

His eyes drifted to hers.

"This actually happened?" he asked with growing consternation.

"It did. In fact, our magnanimous, mostly male-dominated governances at the time, had been provided with creditable projections twelve months before the event, by astrophysicists around the world, who flagged the matter, showing scientific evidence that Encke might pose a much greater threat than earlier believed. Based on their studies, they suggested that there might be larger pieces of the comet, obscured in its trail, not just small fragments, but rocks which could be devastating to Earth, and that such bodies, given their proximity to Earth could be pulled off their normal trajectory by Earth's gravitational field. They strongly recommended a collaborative effort to protect our planet from that possibility." She waved a hand to the air, accentuating her point. "Naturally, as with most things that don't line their pockets or bank accounts or aggrandize their egos, our governing powers put the matter on the backburner, assigned some committees to further study the matter and did nothing effective about the warnings, because, as usual, men were too busy doing what men do." Her words now seethed with a caustic bite.

She walked to the window nearby and looked out into the night.

As she spoke, her voice echoed back to him with a haunting tinge this time. "It is pathetic when you think about it. We had the capacity and technology to defend our world from those rocks. There were well over 15,000 nuclear weapons in the combined arsenals of just nine nations at the time. In fact, we had enough right here in the USA to stop those rocks, and yet, the men in power, men who certainly had no qualms about using those weapons against people, only managed to fire off a handful of them in some placid attempt to intercept those rocks when it was already too late to stop them."

She turned and returned to the Visio and then flicked the image of Earth with a finger, spinning it like a globe. "The first asteroid struck here," she stopped its spin and pointed, "just southwest of Japan's lower island. The second asteroid," she spun the globe once again, "landed in Siberia, on the lip of the East Siberian Sea." Her finger tapped the spot.

Her eyes remained transfixed, as if momentarily mesmerized, and then, slowly, they drifted up to meet his. "No one really knows how big each rock was, best-guess estimates put them at over a kilometer in size. But we certainly know the effects they had when they hit."

She tapped the Visio, working a digital panel within and then continued to walk the room as a montage of images and video clips flashed in front of his eyes.

"Japan disappeared under a tsunami that washed over the islands and wiped out over 140 million people in less than thirty minutes. The coastal regions of China, Southeast Asia and all the islands in between, including the Philippines, experienced tsunamis which eviscerated whole cities, with some two and a half billion people wiped off the face of the Earth by that one rock alone, all in a matter of the time it took for a wall of water taller than the Empire State Building, to travel from the epicenter, destroying everything in its path."

Tanner was speechless, his face pale and his eyes glossed over with shock, as he watched the simulation which showed the spiking waves, as the Pacific Ocean rose, like a beast from the depths of Hell, sending a mountain of water radiating outward and swallowing up whole islands and masses of humanity in the maws of a watery death.

"Now, Siberia," she points to the Visio, "that one really takes the cake. Not only did the shock waves from that impact level a region the size of Texas, and several Russian cities which crumbled, like sandcastles, in its wake," she casually swiped her hand over the Visio, revealing another graphic rendering of the planet "this is what the world looked like within days of the Siberian impact."

He stared at the muddy cloud, a gloomy fog that enveloped the entire globe."

"Are you familiar with Krakatoa?" she asked.

He nodded. "The island in the South Pacific that erupted back in the late 19th century."

"1883 to be exact. Krakatoa was a volcanic eruption that expelled enough smoke and particulates into the atmosphere to darken the skies of the world for five years. In fact, it resulted in climate changes. That was just one volcano, Tanner; so, you can only imagine what happened when two asteroids the size of Lower Manhattan, hit us?"

She sat in her chair and watched him for a time – the placid and empty look on her face betraying the fact that she felt no empathy for his pain.

"While you and your crew were safely tucked away in hibernation, we endured an event which very nearly wiped us out. We estimate four billion deaths just in the aftermath of those two impacts. It took three years for the sediment to settle to the Earth and for the blue skies to return, and in the interim, farming and food production were severely hampered by radical shifts in climate, and we lost countless millions to starvation and disease."

"However, it was the virus that really put the icing on the cake."

Tanner was still trying to reconcile the magnitude of destruction caused by the asteroids.

"What virus?"

"The one that put men on the endangered species list, of course," she said, finally permitting a smile to grace her lips. "When that rock hit Siberia, it not only created the largest and deepest crater on Earth, but it also unleashed a passenger it had been carrying from whatever part of the Universe, a very deadly virus – one that we had never experienced before then."

She drew the Visio to her with a pinch of her forefinger and thumb, and then with a swipe, she shifted the projection with a new simulation.

"The impact flushed tons of ice particulates into the atmosphere, as you can see here," she nodded. "Within days the virus had suffused the globe. We had no idea it existed until the body count started piling up."

"What does it do?" he asked, his mouth now dry as the knot in his stomach became tangibly painful.

She stabbed her finger into the Visio, its long-polished nail sweeping across a screen visible to her.

"That is the human genome. Twenty-three pairs of chromosomes, or forty-six chromosomes in total, right?"

"Not my specialty, but I'll take your word for it."

She offered a condescending grin. "The XX pair in the set is what defines the attributes of the female: the XY chromosome pair, the male. Without getting too technical, the virus is attracted to the male genome, like bees to honey. It hosts on the male DNA, feeding off your body, and as the body fights back with its natural defenses, the immune system starts to weaken, and eventually, it hits a threshold where it can no longer endure. And that is where the deaths start piling up."

Tanner's head was shaking with a life of its own, while incredulity was written on his face like craters pockmarking the moon.

"Men started dying from the common cold, flu and other viruses they would normally have been able to easily endure." She paused with a demure look on her face, unaffected by the gravity of her narrative. Tapping the Visio once again, she produced charts showing the apocalyptic and exponential death toll.

"We could not even keep up with the body count; in fact, we did not have time to do more than ID the corpses, cart them off to incinerators and burn them to protect ourselves from rot and disease. Meanwhile, we were working day and night to keep things together, because with so many deaths and men falling like flies, we had to take over all the functions that fell into neglect."

"And women, they weren't they affected by this virus?"

She shrugged. "The virus did not affect our physiology. Maybe that was God's plan – maybe he designed us to be the stronger of the genders?" A devilish grin spread across her lips.

"I doubt that," he said with a hushed grumble.

She continued with a cavalier and self-satisfied tone. "It would appear that our genetic blueprint, which gives us breasts, a vagina instead of a penis, estrogen instead of testosterone, the strength to bear children and endure childbirth, the subtle weave of our DNA thread compared to yours, somehow blocked the viral attack which feasted on males."

He leaned forward, looking her in the eyes. "But how does this virus affect …"

She cut him off, as if anticipating his question.

"You mean men's ability to reproduce?"

He nodded.

"The virus attacks your XY chromosome, Tanner – essentially, it destroys that part of your DNA." She flicked a casual brow. "Essentially, men were rendered impotent."

"And you've tested this?"

She threw a hand to the air, another gesture of her authority. "Teams of geneticists and scientists pored over this problem for years. Every single man assessed was found to be infected, and every single one of them was also found to be impotent as far as reproduction goes…" she lingered, letting her words seep into his already confused mind.

"The only reason the gender is alive today, and didn't perish at the hands of the virus, is because we finally found a cocktail to hold it at bay, and because of sperm banks around the world which were spared the onslaught of the virus in their cryogenic storage vaults, we've been able to spawn new infants." She spun a slow dance in front of him. "Today, we artificially inseminate women who want children, and of course, if they want, they can still engage in the act of sex with men purely out of lust, but there are no children in the process." She stopped in front of Tanner, declaring her next words with a stoic look.

"And unless we find a way of stopping that virus and reversing its effects, I'm afraid that the future of our race is on the clock – because when the sperm runs out, so does the clock."

"What is this cocktail you mentioned?" he asked, feeling sick to his stomach, as if someone had just punched him in the solar plexus countless times.

"You're familiar with nanotech, I assume?"

Tanner nodded. "Synthetic nanobots."

"We created a nanobotic injection using preprogrammed microscopic robots capable of keeping the virus at bay."

"But it's not a cure?"

Her head shook. "No cure has been found, Tanner, and as far as we can tell, the virus never leaves the body. As a result, the male stamina has been affected as well."

"What does that mean?"

"Think of it as having a cold or flu for the rest of your life. The virus holds the body captive and keeps it in a sort of weakened state."

"So, they have to get the injections regularly?"

She waved her hand theatrically in a wide circle.

"The spores are everywhere around us, Tanner, and no one knows for sure if they will ever disappear from our world. Since the nanobots eventually wash out of the body as waste – regular injections are critical."

"And if they don't get more injections?"

"Then, you die," she answered with a demure and misplaced smile on her lips.

5

Lady V abruptly, and without announcement, exited the room, leaving Tanner steeped in the soup of countless questions; a turmoil of an emotional storm and the feeling that he was tumbling down a very deep, dark hole.

It was not the impact of the asteroids that disturbed him so much – although that was shocking enough, because NASA, in their pre-launch training, had briefed them on the contingency of such events happening. He clearly recalled that astrophysicists who provided the briefs to NASA and ESA, unanimously agreed that Earth was as vulnerable as pins on a bowling alley just waiting for the Universe to pitch a lucky strike.

What really rocked his boat was the fact that men had been nearly eviscerated from the world, in fact, if she was telling the truth, it seemed as if the only men left were now crutched and weakened.

He played their conversation over and over, again, thinking as he did that this "President" was a strange bird; a mix of narcissism, arrogance, and dismissiveness; and even though those qualities were nothing new considering the incumbents of that office back in his day; there was also that constant thread of repugnance she displayed, evident in her attitude whenever she spoke about men. She was not a fan of his gender.

His thoughts were vanquished as the door opened, and once again, she entered the room with the same pompous and dictatorial stride – as if she were strutting on the red carpet before a sea of paparazzi.

She lowered herself into the same chair and smiled at him with a slight cock of her head. "So, Tanner, you still look shocked."

"Wouldn't you be if the shoe was on the other foot."

She shrugged. "Possibly, but the shoe is on the right foot, as Nature intended."

Tanner leaned forward. "Why are we under arrest?"

She touched a finger to her lip, slowly caressing it as she pondered her answer. "Let me you ask you a question, why did you go on a mission that would require sixteen years of your life?"

"The challenge," he shot back – feeling as if she was purposely doing a Segway.

"Computer - show me the profile for Tanner McNeal."

As the document appeared in the Visio, she flicked a hand, spinning it around for him to see."

“Your NASA shrink concluded that you were a loner – a wolf apart from the pack, and that you displayed a deep, but hidden disenchantment with society.” She eyed him with an amused look. “He even recommended that you not be sent on the mission, and certainly, not as its captain.” She raised a challenging brow. “Why did he conclude that, Tanner?”

Tanner shrugged. “I was tired of watching reruns on Netflix?! What is your point?”

“My point is that you didn’t just go into space for the challenge, I think you went to get away.” She stood and circled the Visio, like a wolf circling its next meal.

“I studied your background. American father, Dutch mother, a violent marriage, childhood abuse, divorce; all the classic ingredients for the social outcast, the recalcitrant, the independent and defiant personality.” Her eyes darkened momentarily as she lingered on her last words. “A young boy ends up in foster care and learns how to fend for himself and then becomes an impressive test-pilot, and eventually gets to spin his spurs on the most ambitious space mission ever undertaken. I find that fascinating.”

Tanner shook his head. “Get to the point?”

“I’m just trying to understand the man, what motivates someone to commit to such a sacrifice.”

“I liked the idea of exploring space – the unknown.”

"Or it was more about escapism – an opportunity to get away?"

Tanner glared at her. "Why don't you just say it and stop beating around the bush?"

She cast a dismissive hand to the air and with a smug smile, answered. "Now you're just being rude."

"I want an answer to my fucking question, why are we locked away like common criminals."

Her eyes narrowed as she lashed back, her voice suddenly spiking and cutting the air like the slash of a sword. "Because you are criminals!"

The tension between them vaulted, becoming thick and cold as ice.

With a measured gait, she dragged her chair and straddled it in front of him – her eyes level with his. "You don't know what happened, do you?"

By now Tanner was really confused.

Her head shook with a look of incredulous disdain. "Before you judge people you should make sure you know the truth," she said with a pause, the look in her eyes showing her mental drift. "It was my eighteenth birthday when the sirens went off in our small town in Jersey." She paused as the memories now flooded in from the dark recesses of her mind. "No one really knows why that idiot, Ping-Pong, in North Korea, decided to launch a nuclear assault; maybe he got tired of the constant provocations from our illustrious President who glamorized using nuclear weapons because provoking others was the high point of his skill set. Anyhow, Ping-Pong fired two nukes at us, and two more at South Korea. Our defenses easily intercepted them without casualty before they reached our coast. The Chinese stepped in and managed to shoot down the one headed for Seoul; but the fourth one made it through every counter-ballistic system, and the city of Busan, in South Korea, and millions of people, give or take a few hundred thousand, disappeared in a cloud of radioactive dust."

She drew a deep breath and let it pass her lips slowly. Her eyes darkened in step with the memories now pressing in.

"What do you think happened after that, Tanner?" She looked up at him, expectantly.

"I do not know. We had a com-blackout for most of the mission."

"I heard about that. Well, care to take a wild guess?"

"He reciprocated."

"Bingo! In fact, he not only reciprocated, but he also ordered a full-scale nuclear assault against North Korea. He had just been waiting for a chance to increase his public ratings by showing that he could start a war; something that lousy Presidents like him, who could not lead an army of ants, found easy to do," her words seethed.

"This, Tanner," she pointed, "is what Pyongyang and several other cities in North Korea, look like today."

Tanner's eyes were glued to the horrid images that passed by, showing entire cities reduced to complete rubble, mere ghost towns; the skeletal remains of a conflagration, an inferno that had scorched all life within.

"North Korea does not even exist anymore; those who survived the bombs fled to China, South Korea or even Russia. The radioactive fall-out infected and killed millions of people in neighboring China, Russia, and resulted in sickness throughout Asia and Europe." She waited, watching his face, seeing the ripples of pain and shock taking hold. "So, you see, Tanner," her tone sounded both disparaging and condescending, "America didn't just efface a whole nation, it tipped the dominos, a storm that raged across the globe."

"Here's the irony of it all," she continued with a wave of her hand. "You'd think that because Ping-Pong fired the first shot, that the world would see him as the bad guy in this narrative, but in fact, we were perceived as the real enemies, the murderers, the aggressors, the monsters, because people expected better from America."

"Russia, China, Pakistan – all of them affected by the fall-out, put their entire nuclear arsenals on ready-alert. No one trusted the United States anymore. We lost our position as *guardians of peace and democracy*."

By now, Lady V was pacing the room, her eyes fixed to the floor as a wash of passion effused from her. Finally, she stopped as a smile crept across her lips. “I think the moral of the story is quite laughable – don’t you?”

“Meaning what?” he asked.

She waved a hand to the air. “Men! You finally got what you deserved.”

“You’re saying that women had nothing to do with that mess?”

She tipped her head at him with a brutally challenging glare. “For a guy who captained a crew from here to Jupiter and back you’re short a few marbles, aren’t you?” Her eyes narrowed. “Let me fill in the blanks for you, Tanner. At the time those nukes went airborne, less than 10% of the nations in the world were headed by women; and not one of those women had the power to unleash that kind of hell.”

“You make it sound as if men are wired to be destructive, when the ones responsible are a minority at best.”

A look of pure, unalloyed disgust now reflected in her eyes. “Tanner, Tanner, Tanner, do not play that card with me. History is witness to the truth and you know it too.”

“What truth?”

“Men make war, not women. Men build war machines and weapons of mass destruction, not women. Men walk into schools and shoot kids up, not women. Men run the streets in gangs, killing, raping, and pillaging – women do not do that. Men run human trafficking rings, not women. Men kill. Men murder. Men rape. In fact, statistical studies across the world prove that men committed over 95% of all brutal crimes throughout history – that's indisputable fact." She paused, her eyes now seething with a passion that betrayed a hidden pool of hatred.

"Do you recall any infamous NAZI figures who were women? Do you remember the names of any women who were shooting Jews in the back of the head or committing atrocities during the Holocaust? Name one woman that started and engaged a pogrom to wipe out a whole race of people?" She shook her head at him. "You cannot, can you? Because the infamous characters who screwed up the world were men, and while there a handful of notable women may have played a role in coaching them, or pandering to their power, or spreading their legs for them, they did not officiate the tragedies."

She turned and walked to the far wall and then, leaning against it, folded her arms across her chest with a look of imperious authority on her face. "Men very nearly put us on the path of World War III, a war that would have destroyed the world." She pointed a finger at him. "A handful of nuclear weapons caused that much destruction, so imagine what would have happened if Russia, China and the others had joined the party?"

"That's conjecture."

"Is it?" She approached. "We found transcripts, in the wake of the *Cataclysm*, as men were off dying by the millions and could no longer protect their guarded secrets, both in the Pentagon and their equivalents in Russia, China and elsewhere, showing that their leaders were preparing for nuclear war. You think they cared if millions or billions died, Tanner?" She shook her head. "They didn't; because they knew they would survive it, and in the end, the minority, the rich, the entitled, the bankers and corporate moguls, the oligarchies that ruled the world, would swoop in and scoop up the property and the broken nations, just like they did in World War II, and start over again, only more powerful than before."

She lingered with a wag of her head. "You just do not get it, do you, Tanner. Why build tens of thousands of nuclear weapons if you are not going to use them eventually? The Cold War was not just a stand-off between global powers, held at bay by nuclear bombs, it was just foreplay for the inevitable theater, the day when a dipshit with a dysfunctional ego, would press the little red button. And, unfortunately, the timing was right, we had two stupid-fucks in power at the same time."

She watched the abject confusion that engulfed his face. "You know why I really called you here and why I wanted to personally tell you this?"

"No."

She stepped closer, close enough for him to see the ravages of hatred that roiled deep in her eyes.

"I wanted you to hear it from me, I wanted you to feel our pain, what we endured because of the patriarchal culture that no longer exists."

"You really believe that all men are accountable?"

She tossed a hand to the air with an incredulous shake of her head.

"We are wired differently than you, Tanner. Our impulse is to birth and nurture the race, not to destroy it." She paused to take a calming breath and continued with an amused smug look. "Admittedly, we can be back-stabbing and manipulative bitches, especially to one-another, and power-plays are certainly not beyond us, but…" she pointed a finger at him, "… that is a defense mechanism we have been forced to adopt in a male-dominated culture, one where we had to learn how to adapt and survive and excel despite the power-hierarchy that favored men throughout history."

She watched him for a moment and then she pressed on.

"You not only back seated us as women, but you also constantly treated us as something to control, something to fuck, something to objectify and subjugate, and something to own." She glared at him, her nostrils nearly flaring with repressed rage. "Those days are over, Tanner McNeal. Men will never dominate this world again."

"So, you're telling me all this just because it makes you feel good?"

She dismissed his comment with a flick of her wrist.

"Do you know what the *Inhumane Act* is, the one you and your men have been charged with?"

He shook his head.

"It's a universal manifesto put together by a summit of world leaders on the 4th anniversary of the *Cataclysm*." She turned to face him with a stoic and dictatorial demeanor now pasted to her face as she called up the Visio with the manifesto in clear view.

"That universal declaration was unilaterally accepted by all nations, which decrees that all nuclear arsenals are to be destroyed, and never replenished except as needed for planetary defense against more falling rocks; that military presence is to be reduced to 3% or less of its former size in every nation, and used only as a collective defense system for global good and not for war or profit; that no nation, sovereign or government is ever permitted to invade the borders of another under any circumstances and that in doing so criminal prosecution will be enforced on its leaders by the international courts; that carbon emissions, use of fossil fuels, pollution by plastic and other sources of global warming, be ceased and immediately replaced with sustainable and environmentally friendly means only; that women, everywhere, be granted their inalienable rights; and finally…" she declared with a visage that was a mix of both pride and hate, "… that men, by virtue of their heinous and criminal acts against humanity, both in using nuclear weapons against innocent people, and in permitting those rocks to hit us because of their flagrant neglect of the power entrusted to them, be collectively reduced to a lower status in society, and never permitted the right to lead, to hold any positions of power or authority or governance – ever again."

Tanner huffed. "If what you're telling me is true, there can't have been that many men left, anyhow."

A light shrug touched her shoulder. "True, by that time, four years after the virus spread, we estimated that over 95% of men had died off and more would follow, but it didn't change the principle of the law – that men could never be trusted with power again, because with it, they either destroy or they neglect their responsibility to the people."

"And what makes you think that women will do a better job?"

"Oh," she pranced, nearly cheering herself on, "we are already winning that race, hands-down," she flashed a broad smile as if once again posturing in front of the cameras. "No wars have been waged since the *Cataclysm* and not a single country invaded. Since that time there has been no terrorism, murder-rate has dropped to nothing; rapes and sexual violence are unheard of, crime has reduced to petty misdemeanors at best, global-warming index has dropped by over half of what it was, on and on and on." She waved a hand to the air, "Take any index you want, and you will find that all the negative factors afflicting the world before the *Cataclysm*, are either gone, or nearly so." She paused.

"Possibly the most important thing for us is that we don't have to fight for our relevance anymore in a preferential power-structure patriarchy."

She stepped closer looking him hard in the eyes. "You had your chance, Tanner. Men could have done it right. They could have had peace and prosperity too. They could have saved us from global warming. They could have given us equal share in the game, but they did not, and for whatever reason, you just do not change your ways. So, no, you do not get to fuck up the entire world and the entire human race and then demand a second chance. That is why you are being tried and that is why you and your men are incarcerated, as criminals, because that is what you are."

"So, this is really all about power, isn't it?"

"Everything is about power, Tanner. It is just a question of how that power is used and by whom." She pointed to a poster on the wall. "No doubt, you've seen our motto."

"Hard to miss," he answered.

"Let me show you something," she led him to the window. He stepped next to her, while the two guards followed close behind, their weapons ever ready. "Do you recognize that building?" she pointed to a structure in the distance.

As his eyes adjusted to the darkness, the dim lights splashed an eerie and faint glow over the familiar sight.

"The White House," he answered, shocked by its decadent appearance.

A smile formed on her lips. "It is an empty shell today, Tanner. It has not been used since those rocks hit us. In fact, if you look down the National Mall, you will notice something else is missing."

His eyes worked the terrain, but long absence had dimmed his memories. He looked at her with a questioning face.

"The Washington Monument, of course?" She snickered.

He looked back, and sure enough, the massive and towering obelisk, symbolic of the nation's hard-won freedom and fight for independence, was gone.

She turned to him with a smug look. "I wanted you to hear it from me. It is a new world now, Tanner. Women are in control, and it is going to stay that way."

-III-

1 Eight months later ...

Staring up at a ceiling constructed of faded wooden laths, Tanner's eyes idly traced the pattern in the dim light of his dorm.

It was an exercise in distraction; a monotonous and mindless regimen that helped him escape the dreaded mediocrity of his existence.

His mind maundered, like the ebb and flow of tides, to a distant place, a landscape embraced by both brutal and primordial antiquity, a desolate and remorseless world, and yet, one so spiritually transcendent to any other, that despite its visceral existentiality, it was still quintessentially more connective to his soul than any other place.

There were times, so many times, while on Europa, where he dreamed of coming back to Earth, just to experience its blue skies again, the freedom to breathe its air, to smell flowers and trees, to watch pretty girls passing by on a beach or stand before a cold northerly wind slapping him in the face. And yet, even now, the small planet, despite having none of those merits, still beckoned him; its voice echoed back hauntingly, reminding him that it remained a singularity in a lifetime of experiences; a filamentous bond to a universe so deep, wide, and expansive that just thinking about it infused him with the taste of freedom again.

His three years on the icebound world had exposed a massive and depthless hole inside his soul, a vacancy which he previously sensed, but which Europa had ripped open.

Every time he had sat, alone, staring out into the brutally white landscape of her face, pondering the big questions about existence, questions that had never been answered by any biblical narratives, Big Bang models and certainly not Darwin's monkey-to-man theory – the moments had always left him with a profound sense of connectivity to something bigger.

Here on Earth, it was easy to pitch pet-ideas and beliefs about existence, but out there, on the desolation of a small planet that spun around a behemoth, truth was not a luxury, it was as naked as the blistering cold and the depthless expanse of the canvas that formed the very backdrop of the cosmos.

Footprint.

He sighed just thinking the word. The greatest discovery of their mission lay hidden away in the banks of the ship's computer; infallible proof that another race of beings had visited our solar system sometime in the past.

Where they were from?

How long ago had they visited?

How advanced were they?

Did they know we existed just a stone's throw from Europa?

The questions had stirred his soul, then, and even now, as he lay on his bunk bed.

A slow sigh emitted, as reality crowded back in and replaced his maundering, reminding him that he was a prisoner, that Europa and even *Footprint*, were just memories clouded by the touch of a surreal world.

Today, they were worker-prisoners, incarcerated, and watched by guards and killer drones, a forced life of servitude working the mines. If escape was even possible, they had not figured out a way yet.

A small army of drones patrolled the camp, and they were lethal, something they had all witnessed when a man had attempted an escape one morning. The drone was on him in seconds, firing a pellet into the back of his head with a barely audible puff – killing him instantly.

All he had now was hope, the dim rays of light at the end of a very dark tunnel, and Tanner was not about to give up on that – nor was he going to forget his promise to Telanthia.

2

The staff cafeteria, located on the twentieth floor of the forty-eight-story structure, was buzzing with the voices of hundreds of women.

TDC, short for ***Tetra-Drone Corporation***, the multi-national and global manufacturing giant of robotics in the world, was also Lady V's baby. Not only was *TDC* producing the most advanced Ai robotics on the planet, those used as Lady V's national policing force, but it was a massive cash-cow too.

All considered it to be a great honor, not only to be pushing the envelope on Ai or Artificial Intelligence, but to be working as part of their iconic leader's dream-team.

Telanthia had a different spin on it. As she sipped her coffee, listening to the idle chatter of women nearby, those who worked somewhere in the bowels of the behemoth that formed the tapestry of Manhattan's skyline, she found herself annoyed by all of it.

It was not that she disrespected them, or considered herself better than the other women, it was the fact that they were worlds apart. She had come from a different age, and the new Utopia simply did not fit into her mindset or moral compass.

Ever since the humiliating trial, the so-called Tribunal, Tanner, and the guys had disappeared from their lives. Eight months had passed, and she had not heard a word about them, only that they had been placed at a mining camp somewhere.

During their integration period to the *New America*, the three of them had been brought up to speed on the culture, the expectations of a woman today, the laws that governed the land, moreover, the new status of the male gender.

Each had undergone tests to determine their strongest skill set. Camilla, being an IT genius, was selected to be part of a design team, where her ability could best be used in the creation of new and better Ai. Rose, a quantum specialist and Tel, a microbiologist, were each assigned to a specific division of *TDC* that studied physiology and behavioral adaptation in the field of robotics – in other words, how to make a machine look and act human.

Although no one had stated it, she was sure that Lady V wanted them working somewhere she could keep an eye on them – and what better place than *TDC*, where over six thousand women, a sea of loyal and devout eyes and ears, surrounded them.

It was tiny things that tipped her off to the fact that eyes were on them, such as the odd stares, the occasion when she would see someone looking at her or even at Camilla or Rose; or the raised brows when they went off to a corner of the cafeteria to take a coffee together. There was no doubt that they were under the microscope. Lady V did not trust them? Whatever the reason, she sensed that their freedom was as tenuous as threads of fine silk, a freedom that could be ended summarily if either of them displayed the slightest disaffection toward the regime.

“Did you see his face when I squeezed his butt,” her voice echoed vociferously, followed by loud raucous laughter as a table of women nearby burst out. It was commonplace to hear women talking derisively about men, about how nice their asses were, or the size of their penis, or even lurid details of sex with one, as if the act of intimacy had now been reduced to a mere circus show.

On the other hand, it reminded her of a time when men did the same to her and other women.

The cultural dichotomies were almost surreal to witness in such a brief time.

While a part of her, the female ego, tugged at her mind, trying to reconcile this new world as something good, as a balancing of power, she could not let go of the fact that despite any of its merits, the New America was just another color of discrimination and gender-abuse, the flipside of the coin she once knew.

Being a scientist and behavioral specialist, she tried to analyze her surroundings in an objective sense.

Most of the women at *TDC* were young, and because of that, they were victims and survivors of the *Cataclysm*, a majority of whom had lost brothers, fathers, uncles and more. It was an event so globally traumatizing that the transformative mindset had become normalized.

Men had not only failed the world, they had nearly set it on fire; and according to general census, they had also failed to protect it against those rocks when they had more than enough punch in their hidden arsenals to obliterate them before they threatened the Earth. Moreover, the gender was on its way out – a dying breed, and it was women who stepped in, picked up the pieces, and put the world back on track.

Naturally, the superiority complex was infectious, and with leaders like Lady V reminding them over and over through her media-controlled propaganda machinery, the age of men was over.

Tel's eyes fell on the large poster that adorned one wall – one of many which could be seen around the building, in fact, adorning billboards and the sides of other buildings throughout the city.

A hushed sigh escaped her lips.

She had often wondered why it was that Lady V had made such a spectacle of Tanner and the other men, parading them through a demoralizing Tribunal, a brutal character assassination which the whole nation had watched. But then it came to her one day; Lady V was afraid of Tanner. That was why she had spent so many hours talking to him in private. She wanted to understand the man she feared, because here was a man who had championed humanity by pushing the envelope on space exploration. Someone who could threaten her hold on power.

3

It was a dismal existence for every man in the camps, not just Tanner and his crew.

When they emerged each day from the depths of their sunless tomb, twilight was already fading into darkness. Moreover, their skin was tarnished with the soot of coal, a filmy layer that never seemed to wash off, and their eyes watered in a vain attempt to eviscerate the slime which clung to them.

The barracks were filled with the sound of men coughing and hacking, the result of constant exposure to coaldust which lined their lungs. Even though they were being injected with nanobots to repel the effects of the virus, it did nothing to prevent the steady attrition of their vital organs as a result of the mining, and men were dying as the black death took its inescapable toll on them.

Tanner was desperate for a way to escape their prison. He had no idea what that would accomplish in terms of changing anything in the world, but he knew for certain that he was not going to die inside these walls, and neither would his men.

One day, deep inside a tunnel; separated from the watchful eyes of roving guards, and for that matter, the drones, which constantly swept the tunnels like silent sentries, the Serbian, Matis, edged closer to where Tanner chipped away at a vein of coal. "I think I found a way out of this shithole," he whispered.

Tanner twisted his head, his eyes suddenly aglow. He wiped the black dust that clung to his lips like a leprous scab. "How?"

Matis glanced nervously over his shoulder. "Every day when we enter the mine there is a team of engineers hunched over a table reviewing plans of the shafts we are digging. I have tried to get a looksie, but they are guarded." Matis smiled, his white teeth shining against his coal-black skin. "This morning they were careless. I noticed an air shaft that goes north-eastward, through the mountains we are digging. The opening is actually around the next bend from the tunnel we are in." He grinned.

"You mean, a natural air shaft?" asked Tanner.

"Yeah, that's how we get our air supply down here."

"How far does it go?"

Matis shook his head. "I'd say it runs for at least a kilometer or two."

"You think we can get out through that?"

Matis shrugged. "Don't know, but it's certainly better than shoveling shit in Louisiana."

Tanner nodded. "That's for sure."

4

Lady V stepped from her palatial bathroom, catching her image in the full-length mirror as she did.

She lingered, admiring the gentle curves of her nakedness, the slender lines that defined the supple and provocative shape of her breasts, the smooth twist of her waist and the slim neckline that ended at her powerful jawline.

The sight of herself evoked a smile and a sense of renewed power, the raw unabated mastery of being a woman.

It had taken years for her to reach the point where she could look at herself again, at her full self, at all the sexual nuances of her femininity, and accept the quintessential and visceral strength of her natural endowment.

For years, she felt subdued about it, to the extent that she felt guilty about being feminine, held back by the memories and trauma of his grotesque abuse.

Back then, even in the early years of the Reform, as she began to build up her party, the ***WIP***, ***Women in Power***, she had been constantly ghosted by the haunting specter of his face, his calloused and brutal hands roving over her body as if he owned it, hurting her, feeling her in places that no man should trespass upon a child.

But all of that was in the past – today, she was a powerful symbol of what women truly are and can and should be.

She was free of him, free of men, in fact, men answered to her now.

A smile touched her lips in the thought that soon, Woman EX would change everything, and then men, what few remained, would know what it feels like to be nothing – truly nothing at all.

5

It was Deptha, usually referred to by others as Dep, the ship's scientist, geological specialist, and native Hindu from Mumbai, who had spent countless thousands of hours chipping away at rocks on Europa, who produced a brilliant plan to formulate their escape.

Dep had discovered a small vein of sulfur at the end of one shaft where they worked; and given that sulfur, mixed with coal and a little potassium nitrate, provided all the ingredients necessary to create good old-fashioned blasting powder – it provided the necessary element to their plan.

The plan was laid. Dep would carve out a hole inside a large vein of coal, pack in the sulfur and the potassium nitrate, a pile of which they found at the end of one tunnel, rig a fuse using remnants of blasting coil found amidst the rubble of recently-opened shafts – and voila, big bang.

The others would be waiting near the ventilation hole when the explosion occurred, and if all went according to plan, the collapsed shaft, the very one where Tanner and his team were supposedly working at the time, would not only create a blockade which could take days to dig out, but hopefully it would also be assumed they had been buried in the aftermath.

With nerves at a breaking point, Tanner and his men went about their work as usual, but in each case, they drifted incrementally toward the same location, just beneath the vent.

When the explosion occurred, it rocked the tunnels, sending a tremor that shook the inner-Earth, while casting a shower of dirt and rocks that cascaded down like hard rain, and a billowing cloud of dust which pushed outward like a raging storm.

Dep, came stumbling out of the gray murk, coughing, and choking up dust as he teetered toward them, one side of his face tainted and scorched by the blast.

"Are you okay?" asked Tanner as he gripped the man by the shoulders - shocked by the fresh injury to his face.

"I'll survive," he answered with a grimace.

A flurry of activity erupted in the adjacent tunnels all around them, as the voices of men and guards echoed like screeching ghosts.

Tanner and the others crouched back into a dark nook, a depression, letting the darkness shield them from watchful eyes as guards raced by in the direction of the blast.

Once they passed out of sight, they sprinted for the nearby air shaft, which appeared as nothing more than a small aperture in the rocky ceiling of one ventricle, permitting air to filter down into the bowels of the Earth.

Michael Brenner, a former college football tackle and the largest of them, crouched down below the opening, while the others spring-boarded off his back, clutching a rocky outcrop and pulled themselves up into the shaft.

More shouts erupted as guards could be heard letting out a high-piercing whistle, a sign to everyone in the tunnels to evacuate and congregate at the meeting point outside the mines.

Tanner shoved the last man upward and then followed. Michael Brenner struggled to his feet as the pain in his back gripped him. He reached up as two men clasped his arms and heaved. As they did, they heard the pounding of approaching feet.

"Pull," commanded Tanner, and together they drew the heavier man up, his feet clearing the aperture just a split-second before more guards and drones swept into view.

6

"Hey there, girls," the screechy voice accosted their ears as Betty waltzed into the cafeteria and came to a stop in front of Tel, Rose, and Camilla, who sat eating lunch.

"What'chya eat'n," the brassy loudmouth from Queens asked as she plunked herself in a chair across from them with a sandwich and soft drink.

As much as they found the floor manager, and their boss, distasteful in every way possible, they also knew that maintaining a good face with her was not only smart, but it was necessary if they ever hoped to find their friends. The adage, keep your friends close and your enemies even closer, seemed to ring true for them, especially now in a world entirely dominated by women.

"Salad. You know, watching my waist," answered Tel with a sidelong glance at Camilla and Rose.

"Your waist?!" Betty roared with an arrogant and boastful displacement of air.

"Just want to stay in shape," answered Tel, careful not to say more than necessary. Deep down, she sensed that Betty was a card-carrying loyalist who had been tasked to keep an eye on them and report back on any incongruities.

Betty pointed a finger at her. "You should seriously consider getting yourself knocked up," continued the blonde-haired person, speaking through a mouthful of food. "Doesn't cost much and you can get yourself a certified sperm donor." She munched on her sandwich, speaking as she did. "In fact, there are places where you can hire a man for a night, get a good lay. A girl like you could easily find a good set of balls to have fun with," she eyed Tel with a strange and leering look. "Besides, you ain't always gonna have those perky tits, girl. Best enjoy them while you can," she finished with flick of her brows.

"I appreciate the advice, thanks, Betty."

That, and countless more inane conversations like it, either with Betty or other women they met or worked with, reflected a similar, marginalized, and disconcerting attitude which women now bore towards men.

Men were now regarded as a sub-class of humans, in fact, during their indoctrination to New America, they learned that Lady V had created the ***Classification Bureau***, the **CB**, which decided on the value of men, assigning them to one of three categories in society.

Class-A were those, mostly family or husbands or the like, of women who had survived the *Cataclysm*. These men, or boys at the time, were permitted to attend school, work menial jobs, or stay at home.

Class-B were blue-color workers – laborers in factories and the like.

Class-C worked on farming communities, in mines, or other labor-intensive work outside the urban areas. Those in this class of men were considered criminals – replacing the need for prison systems, because such men lived in guarded facilities anyhow.

Of the relative few men seen walking the streets, whether driving a bus or cab, being a store clerk, or the like, they were always regarded as something less, marginalized as pseudo citizens and mere objects for sex.

For the women who had grown up in the post-*Cataclysmic* period, it seemed natural to see men this way, but to the three former members of the *Dauntless*, it was a constant reminder of a dystopian and Orwellian world they now found themselves in.

Tel made a habit of buying a coffee on her way home, every day, from an elderly man who operated a small street-kiosk. He reminded her of her father, with his silver-white hair, a sea of wrinkles on his face, but eyes which betrayed a world of pain inside, and a friendly smile which he always provided her with when she stopped to briefly talk with him.

Her most recent conversation with the man filtered through her mind as she sat watching Betty chomp down her sandwich like a hungry lion.

"You're different than the others," he said with a cautious glint in his eyes as he handed her a coffee.

"I'm not from around here."

He grinned, his cheeks bunching up the wrinkles into a furrowed row. "You're the only one that ever shows me any respect," he said with a hushed and saddened voice. "I'd nearly forgotten what it felt like to be treated as an equal to others."

Tel bit her lip as tears pooled in her eyes. "I'm sorry it all turned out this way."

He pressed a hand to hers and squeezed it. "It is not your fault, honey, we brought this on ourselves. God is punishing men for our sins."

7

Without light to guide them, the six men, with Tanner in the lead, groped and felt their way along the dark and narrow shaft – one that twisted through the bowels of the mountain like a massive snake.

The walls, molded by countless years of water, were a plethora of sharp and lethal rocks which jutted out at every turn, accosting them, like creatures in dark crevices snapping at their extremities.

Groans and angry expletives could be heard as the rocks took their toll.

Besides being a sheer gauntlet of lethal protrusions, the deeper they went, the hotter and heavier the air became – and sweat poured off them like a river.

They often found themselves trudging through slithering pools of guck, the remnants of water that had collected, and the fetid smell of rot, which sent shivers through them.

It was a constant battle, climbing steep slimy slopes, slipping, bruising, and bleeding, and equally so, on the downward grade. In the depthless black, they saw nothing, and for all they knew, strange creatures, deep in the mountain realm, spiders, or other species, were watching them, waiting for a chance to pounce and levy a mortal sting.

For Tanner, the sense of overwhelming claustrophobia was ever-present. At times, they had to squeeze through spaces that paralyzed him with terror, wondering if at some point, the mountain would simply hold on and never let go.

After an eternity of time, it seemed, bruised, and cut beyond imagination, with hunger, dehydration, and exhaustion besieging them, Tanner stretched his head through a hole twice the size of a man and looked down into a massive subterranean cavern.

Stalactites protruded downward from the cave-top high above, while stalagmites speared upward – like the maws of a Jurassic creature.

High above was an opening, and through it, Tanner could see the blue sky, and from it, he felt the wash of life-giving air which filled his hungry lungs.

They soon navigated the steep decline where they found pools of fresh rainwater captured in stone cavities at the base of the cave. They drank the water and then collapsed, while their stomachs groaned and growled at them – they were starving.

Tanner refused to succumb to sleep as his tired eyes constantly worked the walls of the cave around them, carefully surveying them for the best way to reach the aperture at the top, at least thirty meters above. His search soon fell on what looked like a narrow cleft or ledge, running from one side, following a steep angular path upward.

He pointed. "That's the only way out, guys," his finger followed the rocky outcrop. They groaned in response.

Tanner did not wait to discuss the plan. Time was not their friend right now. The guards would soon discover the truth about their escape, and it would take no time at all for the drones to catch up with them.

Pushing himself to his feet, he felt a tremble in his legs, the shaking of tired and strained muscles. Nonetheless, he started the climb.

The first twenty meters up the side of the cave was beyond harrowing. Gripping stones and small outcroppings, he moved with immense effort, drawing on a well that defied his already exhausted and battered body. Finally, Tanner gripped the ledge and swung himself up, falling onto his back and stared at the opening above as he caught his breath. Then he rolled over and reached a hand to Mav and pulled him over the lip. The process repeated until each man was sitting on the narrow outcrop – their chests heaving and their bodies trembling from exertion.

After a short reprieve, they pressed onward, hugging, and gripping the rocky wall with their cheeks skidding along it crusty surface, with only a small ledge, twenty or thirty centimeters in width, often-times narrowing down to ten or less, providing a bare foothold separating them from certain death if they lost their grip.

Tanner, in the lead, kept his eyes on the small opening above, which, with every step, grew just a little larger. Sweat poured off his body as every muscle and every ounce of his strength and willpower was challenged.

The sound of rock cracking caught the ears of every man, as stone crumbled and fell, shattering in the darkening cave below. They looked back to see the last man, Matis hanging there by one hand, holding onto a rocky outcrop, his body dangling over the place where the ledge had suddenly disappeared from under him.

Michael Brenner eased back, his heart beating hard against his chest as he hugged the wall. He could see the fear in Matis, his face and eyes gripped by the terror of inevitable death just waiting for him.

"Can't hold on much longer," he said, his words coming between broken breaths as exhaustion threatened to catapult him to his death. Just then, Michael reached out a hand and grabbed the smaller man by the arm, jerking him toward him, just enough so that Matis could get a purchase on the ledge.

"Dude, no time to die?" said Michael with a grin.

By the time every man was safely out of the cave, stretched out on the hilltop, panting and trembling, the moon was already in full bloom.

They were free.

8

To the rest of the workers at the mine, the explosion was just another accident, a circumstance that inevitably befell the workers.

Death was as common to them as the rising sun. Every day, someone expired, either by accident, to the ravages of coal dust destroying their lungs, or to the virus.

No one mourned the men who perished, no one really cared, because apathy consumed them in the knowledge that the Grim Reaper would come, eventually, to collect them too. For many, *sooner* was preferable to a lifetime of slavery.

To the investigative team, however, and as the news reached Lady V's ears, the assessment was quite different; Tanner McNeal and his entire crew had escaped.

V sat in her office, a titanic space that stretched the length of one entire side of the penthouse atop the thirty-eight-story building, *The Center*, the new headquarters of the government of New America; an office which mirrored the nature of the person who occupied it.

The other half of the penthouse, equally as large, was customized as her lavish living quarters.

The Presidential office was anything but a warm and inviting place. It was sterile and cold, completely devoid of any trace or veneration for the historical figures who had preceded her as President. In fact, there was not a vestige of the earlier era, as if the nation had begun with her term and not a second before.

Intentionally designed to be austere, its walls were a hue of lackluster gray, like that of imminent twilight. On one wall, and only one, hung a large painting of two flowers in a furrowed field of dirt – one of them blooming with white petals, the other wilting and dying: the allegorical death of one age and the birth of a new one.

Glass, from floor to ceiling, formed one entire wall which overlooked the National Mall; and centered on this backdrop was an equally titanic-size desk, stretching three meters in length, its sharp-edged surface made of polished steel, giving it a lethal aspect.

In the center of the room, inlaid on the marble floor, was the symbol of *WIP - Women in Power* – the hands of a woman breaking the chains of enslavement.

In every respect and nuance, it was a break from the conventions and mediocrity associated with the old world, the patriarchal world of men, the world of a power-hierarchy that no longer existed.

V stared at the building in the distance, the crumbling vestiges of a time come and gone; and like the decadence of the Roman ruins, the White House showed its years of disenfranchisement – no longer the heart and soul of the nation, just another wasted and forgotten structure from antiquity.

She could have had it dismantled, no one would have cared, but its tragically expiring face, its fading lackluster, and the creeping and growing vines which now scaled its formerly pristine facade, was testimony to an age that had expired – and that was a statement to all - the death of an archaic epoch, and the victory of the new age of women.

In fact, victory was her call-sign, as Lady V.

"You're sure they got out through the air shaft?" she spoke to the Visio hovering nearby.

"Yes, ma'am, we've picked up traces of their trail," answered the head of the mining facility.

Lady V quietly seethed. "Deploy drones to scout every inch of that mountain area. If there is an exit from that shaft, I want guards posted there, and they wait until they show up, or until we find them inside."

As the Visio faded, her mind was accosted by a problem. This was not just an escape, like others who had managed to get away and were eventually tracked down. This was Tanner McNeal, a man who presented a creditable background, a man who had traversed millions of miles and survived sixteen years in space, in conditions that defied existence itself; moreover, a man who could lead others – someone she could not permit to be on the loose.

She had plans, and those plans involved releasing Woman EX – and nothing could be permitted to interfere.

9

Huddled in a tight circle inside an old, abandoned farmhouse, with a small fire crackling in a stone hearth, providing, at best, a modicum of heat, Tanner and the others sipped on a warm brew which Michael Brenner had managed to throw together using an old pot, water, and an assortment of spices he found in a drawer. It was not much, but it temporarily appeased the pain in their empty stomachs.

Around them, the ambience of the dilapidated wood structure was a dim reminder of an age that had long since passed.

Its appearance betrayed the fact that it was decades old, even a century or more. Thick cobwebs hung like threaded curtains from every corner and doorway; and the musty scent of forgotten use, the very permeance of death itself, filled the air. It was not a happy place – in fact, it seemed to scream out in pain, as if having been abandoned and forgotten in this tiny patch of woods was brought back to memory by the men now within its embrace.

Tanner's mind was fast at work. All his attention had been focused on escaping the bowels of that mountain, but now, he had to figure out a plan – what next?

Mav laid his cup on the floor and looked at him. "What'chya thinking, Cap?"

"That they probably already have drones scouring the countryside for us."

"Yeah, I figure that is the case. Our body heat signature will show up like a bulb in a dark room, making us easy prey for the drones," added Mav.

Tanner nodded.

"We should camouflage our skin, using dirt or mud," said Brenner who was listening in. "Military

101 – helps to prevent infrared scans from picking up body heat."

"Good idea," said Tanner. "Meanwhile, we need to find weapons."

"What happens if we get caught?" asked Deptha – the burn to his face looking even worse than before. "I wasn't trained in guerrilla warfare," he said with a humble smile.

For a long moment, the group fell silent.

A rat scurried in the darkness nearby – but its presence did not dissipate the morbid thoughts which suddenly pervaded their minds at the thought of the drones hunting them down.

10

As with most days, Tel, Rose, and Camilla would meet up at a small café on their way to work, and there they would sit and have a coffee.

It was a ritual which helped them to endure their captivity and retain sufficient calm to navigate the turbulent waters of their own souls. Here, they could speak freely, although still hushed, without the eyes and ears of TDC employees, not to mention security cameras and drones, which pervaded the building.

"I really hate that bloom'n place," said Rose, her face twisting into a sneer.

"Me too," chimed in Camilla, more conservative in manner, but no less passionate.

Tel took a deep breath, repressing her own emotions which did not differ from theirs. There was little else on her mind than somehow finding Tanner and the guys and helping to free them, but she also knew that going headlong in a rash attempt to do so would not accomplish the result she wanted.

Their years in space had taught her valuable lessons, one of which was that patience was a virtue.

In her earlier life she saw patience as a weakness, not a merit, because it contradicted the mindset of her upbringing in the shadow of the *Gen-Net* or *Generation Net*, and her own, the *Gen-Alphas*, the entitled ones who expected everything to happen immediately, right now, and not a second later.

Patience and tolerance were not its bywords.

In her immutable way, Lady Space had challenged that mindset, brutally so, because out there in the vastness of her domain, the Cosmos, she was boss, and survival depended on making a pact with her and playing by her terms. Necessity to survive sixteen years in space had taught Tel to bide her time, to watch, to observe, to be careful and diligent – because space did not give second chances; all it took was one wrong move, a minor collision, a moment of carelessness or oversight – any one of which could lead to instant death.

They sipped their coffees in silence, watching the passersby, the stream of cars, and of course, the ineffable presence of New York City yellow cabs, a cultural ingredient that could not be effaced from the Big Apple, no matter what holocaust befell the planet.

Camilla broke the solitude. “What do you think is happening to Tanner and the guys?”

Tel’s body tensed as she cast a furtive glance around the café to make sure no one was listening in.

“We all know that none of those men, no matter their circumstances, will remain slaves.”

Rose grinned, a sagely gesticulation as she eyed Tel with a challenging look. “And Tanner?”

Tel raised a brow. “I was speaking about all of them.”

“I know, but the one you’re really worried about is him.”

Tel was silent.

“The mission is over, Tel. You are not bound by NASA’s mandates, so just admit it - you love him, you always have.”

Tel’s eyes drifted discursively to a nearby table where four women sat in social discourse. “Was it that obvious?” she asked as her eyes floated back to look Rose in the face.

Rose smiled as she leaned in. “I am a woman, remember? I’ve got boobs and a vagingo, just like you.” She flicked her brows. “We can see through your camouflage, Tel. We have special radar for that kind of shit."

Tel sighed, wishing that they were back on the *Dauntless*, or even on Europa, because at least there, she was with him – and now all she had were painful memories of seeing Tanner being forcefully taken from her life.

11

With the aid of an old worn map of the Pennsylvania region, one they had found stashed in a cupboard, they soon established that they had exited the airshaft somewhere in the western foothills of the Allegheny Mountains, around New Kensington, Pennsylvania.

Tanner and Mav pored over the chart. They knew they could not stay off the grid for long without being spotted. It was just a matter of time before the drones, or someone, would compromise them. They needed weapons, a means of defense, and they needed food – and they needed them now!

Mav's eyes hitched on something. He placed a finger on Leechburg. "There's an armory there," he announced.

Tanner stared at it for a moment and then he looked up at Mav. "How can you tell?"

Mav grinned. "My dad used to take me to visit armories when we travelled – he was a civil war buff – you know, one of those guys who loved civil war re-enactments and all. Anyhow, that symbol," he pointed, "means there is an historic armory in Leechburg."

"So, what, we're going to fight off drones with muskets?" posed Brenner.

Mav shook his head. "My dad told me that some of these armories were used as real arsenals, with hidden vaults stockpiled with weapons if local citizens had to be mobilized as a militia."

"No, shit, Sherlock!" exclaimed Brenner, his interest now piqued.

Mav nodded. "I'm not talking about muskets and flintlocks, either, I mean, the real stuff."

Tanner pondered it for a moment. "What if V has already dismantled them?"

Mav shrugged his shoulders. "Why would she give a shit about them, there are no men around to fight anymore – right?"

12

It was a pastoral setting; a warm sun lingered in the sky, fields of green, rolling hills and cotton clouds dangled in the air – a moment of perfection, as if captured on a canvas by Monet himself.

Flowers, in a myriad of colors and shapes, flocked together in an ocean of pastel hues, undulating like gentle waves caressing a sea.

As he walked, his palms barely touched their petals, a titillating and absorbing sensation, all the while his eyes remained fixed on the image ahead.

At first it wavered and shimmered, like a faint specter in a hot desert, but then, her shape formed clear against the background, and her snow-white hair blazed in the sun.

When they were within reach of one another, Tel smiled at him, a smile so radiant and so beautiful that it challenged the sun to do better.

She reached out a hand, and just inches from touching his, from expressing their withheld love, her body dissipated, like sand scattering to the wind, and in her place stood Lady V – her eyes probing his, her lips formed in a hateful sneer and her imperious body language taunting him, as if she wanted him to lash out at her, to hate her, to feel as much rage against her as she felt for him.

Tanner awoke with a start.

A hand gripped him by the shoulder as Mav tipped his head at him. “You okay, Cap?”

He sat up, shaking the haunting vision from his mind. “Just a nightmare.”

“Yeah, well, we’ve got company,” he pointed through the small clearing that skirted the stand of trees shielding them.

Tanner focused his eyes on the line of trucks which rolled down the distant road."

"What do you think?" he asked.

Mav shrugged. "They look like the same kind of trucks used to transport us to the mines. I'm thinking they've got men inside."

At that moment, an idea sparked in Tanner's head. They waited throughout the day, fighting off the bite of a brittle autumn air, further aggravated by the constant ache of empty stomachs.

As the last light of the sun faded over the horizon, they prepared themselves for a hike through the Pennsylvania wilderness. While there were roads crisscrossing the domain, which would have made their progress so much easier and faster, everyone knew that the drones would be surveilling those.

Trudging through thick undergrowth and an endless sea of trees and shrubbery in the dark provided its own form of abuse, a trip filled with exclamatory "fucks" and "shit" and "mother fucker!" as shins were bruised, and skin was cut or damaged by hidden obstacles which jutted out and attacked them.

Just before dawn, they crept up to a main road where a tilted and battered sign announced - *Leechburg*.

Tanner glanced to the east, as hues of pink and orange began to spread across the mantle of clouds, shouting of dawn's approach. "Should we risk it?" he said as he turned to the others.

"I say we go now," answered Michael.

"Me too," added Dep.

Petar and Matis nodded their agreement.

Mav just smiled, but that was his way of saying *yes*, because if he did not agree, he would not hesitate to say it.

Despite the short distance to the town, progress was slow. Approaching vehicles repeatedly forced them, face-first, into the wet and muddy ditch paralleling the roadside.

Finally, a worn and forgotten sign announced the armory, standing on a corner plot just off the main road. It was a small one-story structure, built of stone with an aged-timber roof, a complete throwback to the colonial and revolutionary days of America – obviously, an historic site, and mostly forgotten about judging by its decadence.

Mav dashed across the road, jumped onto an old wooden banister, and pulled himself up onto the low roof of the armory. He glanced around to make sure no one was near and then with a powerful stomp of his heel, he easily broke a hole through the rotting timber, eventually making an aperture large enough to squeeze through.

As the others watched, the sun crept up higher in the sky, its light threatening to expose them as they lay by the road wide open.

Moments later, Mav's head emerged from the door of the building, with a thumbs-up, and not a moment too soon as more cars appeared on the road ahead.

Inside, the armory smelled of mold and rot – the musky odor of antiquity.

Thick dust clung to the glass cases which housed vintage muskets, rifles and other weapons dating as far back as the 1600s; while cobwebs adorned the place, as if someone had purposely designed it that way.

With every step they took it stirred up a cloud of choking dust, a reminder of its destitution.

Mav ran his fingers along the top of the wainscoting.

"What are we looking for," asked Dep.

"A hidden entrance. If there is an arsenal here, there is a trip or a secret door."

The men spread out, their hands rapidly working the walls, door frames and cornices – poking their heads into every closet, and lightly tapping the walls for any sense of hidden cavities within. Finally, a voice erupted. "Got it!" announced Petar as he pulled back a hidden panel disguised as part of the wainscoting. He poked his head into the hole and gasped.

Tanner looked over his shoulder, as did Mav. "Holy mother …!" exclaimed Mav as they looked down into a vault lined with cabinets and shelves that were filled with weapons and military paraphernalia, including a stash of canned foods – more than they could ever have hoped for.

13

V stood looking out over the vista of the city, like an Emperor gazing down at her domain. The sight somehow emboldened her, as if she were drawing energy and power from it.

When she had been voted into office as President, years before, one of her first mandates was that Washington D.C., named in honor of George Washington, a founding father of the nation; whom she considered to be a complete misogynist, would exist no more. From that day forward, she announced, the nation's capital would be called ***The Center*** and America would be referred to as **New America**, to expunge the taste of a nation that had killed millions in the era before hers.

She considered it her city.

She had saved it.

She had rebuilt it.

She was reshaping its very matrix now; and no woman before her had ever sat at the helm of this ship.

"Ma'am," the voice gently cut the air, penetrating her light trance, as the face of her assistant appeared on the holographic Visio.

“What is it?” she turned to face it – annoyed that her silent reprieve had been interrupted.

“There’s been an incident in a small town, an armory was broken into.”

V’s jaws clenched tight. “Where?”

“Leechburg, PA, just northeast of Pittsburgh. They took weapons from a hidden cache.”

V’s subtle fear suddenly sparked and flamed into something bigger. “What kind of weapons?”

“Semi-automatic rifles, ammunition, grenade launchers, assorted military gear and C4 explosive.”

She clenched her jaws so hard that they could have crushed stones at that instant.

14

Working in the dark of night, they prepared the blockade, hauling two large fallen trees from the nearby forest and then propping them up with make-shift trips.

It took hours to prepare, but now, it was just a waiting game as they lay hidden in the grass by the road.

As the sun peeked over the horizon, and the approaching daylight painted a hue of salmon-pink across the sky, the dew formed around them, soaking into their clothes, and making the wait ever more discomforting.

Mav tipped his head at Tanner. "I need to take a piss."

Tanner smiled as he peered through a set of military-grade binoculars which they had shopped from the armory the day before. "Hold onto it, they should be here soon," he said.

"Easy for you to say, your bladder isn't about to explode."

"Don't be such a whiner."

"Yeah, well, when you gotta go, you gotta go," but Tanner cut him off with a jerk of his head as the headlights suddenly appeared in view, coming around the distant bend.

He turned to Mav. "You're on!"

Mav and Matis sprinted across the road, and just in time too, because mere seconds later, a drone came silently gliding by. Its blue neon-light fanned back and forth, systematically scanning the road. Suddenly, it stopped and looped back, hovering precisely over the spot where Mav and Matis had just traversed.

"Shit!" whispered Tanner as he watched the drone hanging in the air; its ocular eye sweeping the area with digital precision.

In the distance, the rumble grew louder as the convoy approached.

The drone remained unmoving, and from his position, Tanner could see that it was onto something, their heat signature, possibly; whatever it was, something was holding its attention.

He knew he had to act fast otherwise their whole plan would fail, and worse, if that drone continued to scrutinize the area, it would eventually find them.

Tanner rolled over on his back, groping in the thick wet grass until his hand gripped a fist-sized rock. With a powerful thrust, he lobbed it into the trees. The drone spun and sped in the direction of the sound.

Only seconds later, the first truck was upon them. They tripped the releases. Two massive tree trunks crashed down and rolled onto the road – blocking the way. The lead truck lurched and fishtailed to an abrupt stop – while the other two also came to a stop behind it.

Suddenly, the drone was back, but Tanner was ready for it this time. He tapped Michael Brenner on the shoulder, and as he did, Brenner, being the best shot amongst them, aimed and fired. The drone exploded in a cloud of metal particulates above them.

They descended on the trucks, and to their surprise, there was only one guard overseeing the whole convoy.

Opening them up, they found scores of men, old and young. They were lean and frail, reminiscent of old-world slave camps, a feebleness about them that could only be explained by the virus which had stolen their manliness.

Tanner looked at the disheveled group, their faces reflecting their utter confusion at what had just happened.

"If you want to be free and you're willing to fight for it, then come with us," he announced. "Otherwise, stay here and go back to being a slave."

The trucks emptied within a minute – not a soul remained behind.

Mav set off into the woods with a parade of others in tow.

Tanner approached the guard, who sat on the roadside under the watchful eye of Matis. He crouched down to look her in the face.

"Tell Lady V that Tanner McNeal sends his regards."

15

Rose suppressed a sardonic grin as a group of women passed by her desk at *TDC*.

Difficult as it was for the quarrelsome Welsher to put up a positive social veneer, she forced an affected look of acquiescence, one which hid the sea of turbulence beneath.

Every day she battled with the bottled-up emotions, the anger, the frustration, the sheer disgust – knowing that if she let the beast out of its cage that it could easily end their chances of ever escaping this Utopic nightmare.

Her current station in life brought back memories of her early twenties, when she worked as an office temporary worker to make extra cash to pay for her flat in the *Highbury* district of London, while studying for a degree as a quantum physicist.

Her final, and radical thesis on theoretical quantum-mechanics as applied to measuring black holes, had caught the eye of a senior NASA scientist who was always looking for fresh, out-side the box, thinkers, and despite her pugnacious attitude and quarrelsome reputation, she made it on the shortlist, eventually winning a seat on the *Dauntless*.

As she watched the faces of women around her, their acquiescence, their unchallenging acceptance of this new paradigm, the only safe port she could find to calm the turbulent waters of her mind was history itself. The Egyptians had done the same thing, as did the Romans, even the great British Empire, all of them had marginalized people under their domain, redefining the rules of the game, mandating false standards which objectified some people as better than others, and then subjugating them to fulfill their sense of entitlement and greed.

Those empires were gone forever.

What she saw around her now, beyond the chrome, beyond the fancy computers, the swanky attire and all the amazing “freedoms” these women cawed and bragged about, as if freedom was now some kind of meme, was a society that had sold-out to the Devil itself – the same deathtrap that marked the eventual demise of every empire that had divided people, making some more equal than others, and thereby breaking the natural order of life.

It was not that she was indifferent to the plight of the sisterhood. Rose had endured the subtle and not-so-subtle inequalities, and the Jurassic mentality of the male-dominated patriarchy she had left behind as they rocketed off into space. Even in those early days back in England, she had seen her share of gender-discrimination. The simple fact that she was a woman with breasts and a vagina and not a penis was a license to alter the terms of engagement.

Her mother had been an inspiration to her in this respect and had confided to Rose that for a woman to excel in the world she needed to be better at what she did than the men around her, because that was how women found their window of opportunity.

Despite that imbalance, Rose harbored no real animosity or grudge toward men. Sure, she had endured her share of sexist remarks, the leers, the derisive comments about her tits being bigger than her brains, the pats on her rump and the not so subtle sexual advances, and the thread of superiority which a certain portion of men felt entitled to leverage in the workplace, but in all, she respected them, because, in spite of their faults, and they certainly had them, men had been a part of her success and her triumphs in life, just as much as women.

She fixed a transient eye on Tel who sat nearby at another workstation. It was a tacit invitation. Moments later, they sat with coffee cups in hand, in the far corner of the canteen, out of earshot of others.

Rose smiled, calculatingly delivering her next words without changing the demeanor on her face, because a sour look, a dissatisfied look, an angry look, was all it took for someone to notice.

"I overheard two security guards talking this morning while I was waiting for the elevator."

Tel forced a smile to her lips, tilting her head at Rose, as if she were listening to her talk about her latest shopping spree.

"Some men escaped from a Pittsburgh mining camp."

Tel's eyes widened with hope.

"There's more," said Rose with a veil of duplicity on her face. "They ambushed a convoy and freed more men." She took a sip on her coffee. "There is a full-scale search going on. The guards are on the high alert right now."

"You heard all of this while waiting for the elevator?"

"Well, to be honest," she grinned impishly, "I did happen to drop something, and missed my elevator so I could listen in some more."

Tel let out a slow and hushed sigh – trying her best to muzzle the torrent of emotion suddenly unleashing inside. Her eyes locked on Rose's face.

"You think it could be Tanner?"

Rose cocked her head. "It's certainly his style."

16

The distant hills were spotted, like fireflies in the night, by the indigo-light of drones scanning the countryside in search of them.

Using the exact point where the convoy had been ambushed as ground zero, and dividing up the land into digital quadrants, each drone sought-out heat-signatures, while transmitting live footage back to the *Central Assessment Bureau*, or *CAB*, the federal agency formed at the behest of Lady V, to provide an umbrella of security for New America, and replacing its defunct ancestors – that is, the CIA, FBI, NSA, Homeland Security, et al, all of which essentially faded into redundancy in the wake of the *Cataclysm*.

It was the largest search-effort undertaken in years, the first time that a group of men, such as these, had escaped and assaulted the regime.

A dozen analysts studied the input from the drones, searching for signs which might reveal the whereabouts of the fugitives.

Lady V sat alone in her office.

Inside she seethed with anger, like the swirl of an ocean vortex, it held her in its grip. Not only had Tanner and the others escaped, and helped others to do the same, he had humiliated her.

His words still rang in her head - *Tell Lady V that Tanner McNeal sends his regards.*

Arrogant bastard! she yelled, plucking a stapler from her desk, and hurtling it into the nearest wall.

Never in her years as the nation's leader had she been challenged like this, especially not by the ilk of men.

She drew a deep breath and released it to calm herself, thinking as she did that Tanner McNeal had proven to be not only an intelligent man, but a cunning, dangerous, and driven one.

As if she were talking to her doppelganger, a mirror-image of herself, she conversed with the voice inside her head. Her alter-ego spoke back to her – as if it were her mentor. It was the same voice that spoke to her that very first night after he left her room, leaving her shaking and trembling from the sexual assault; a voice that returned repeatedly, eventually dominating her thoughts with one thing - that the time was coming when she would exact her revenge.

Despite the humility, the pain, the rage that filled her soul after every encounter, she endured his trespasses. She buried the vision of his ugly face, his putrid and lustful breath, the calloused and cold hands that probed her in areas no child should endure, and the horror of being invaded by a man who was supposed to protect her, not abuse, and rape her.

As the voice faded in her head, the idea came to her.

She tapped the intercom.

“Yes ma’am.”

“Get my jet ready.”

“Destination, ma’am,” asked her secretary.

“New York City.”

17

Tanner knew that it was only a matter of time before the swarm of Ai’s scouring the countryside would detect their presence inside the cave in which they now hid.

Together, with his team, Mav, Michael, Dep and Matis, and with Petar standing watch at the mouth of the cave, they discussed their next move.

“They will find us if we stay too long,” said Dep, his head bobbing side to side, a gesticulation typical of his people. He continued. “The combined body heat of this many men,” he said while casting a glance at those they had freed and who now lay about, slumped over in sleep or simply resting from exhaustion after their escape, “will eventually show up on their infrared-scans. It is unavoidable, and given the advanced sensors on those drones, we are walking a very thin rope right now."

"I know," sighed Tanner with dread painted on his face, "but we need food before we can attempt another run. They," he nodded at the large group of men, "simply won't survive long without it."

"I do have an idea," offered Dep, who had so craftily devised the explosive back in the mines that permitted them to escape. "I can scout deeper into the cave. There must be a vent somewhere, I can feel the draft," he said with a raised finger to the air. Tanner and Mav both shared a shudder as ghostly images of being trapped inside another mountain suddenly accosted them.

"I think I'd rather face the drones," responded Mav.

Dep's head continued to bob. "Nonetheless, I believe my idea has merit."

Brenner hefted the *Kalashnikov Alpha*, the matt-black semi-automatic he had scooped up from the armory. "Tell you what, Dep, you look for an escape route. Me, I'm sticking with my old friend here," he grinned as he held the lethal weapon up in the air. "A forty round-clip, 7.62 caliber slugs, penetrates any body armor. If they corner us, they will be answering to my god," he said with the look of a man who was prepared to fight it out to the death.

Tanner cringed at the thought of Brenner unleashing that firepower at anyone. At the same time, he empathized with him. They were walking a road that no one was prepared to turn back on.

"I think Dep is right," said Mav. "We need all the options we can get – even though the idea of squeezing through dark spaces makes my skin crawl."

"Fair enough," said Tanner. "Give it a shot, Dep."

Dep went off, collecting up necessities - including two men who promptly volunteered to go with him.

Tanner turned to Mav. "You guys pop out while it is dark and see what you can forage up in terms of food. Petar and I will stay behind and ride shotgun."

Tanner watched as both groups headed off; Dep into the bowels of their mountain domain, and Mav and two others, into the dangers of the night. He did not want to think about the consequences that Dep might encounter a dead-end or even the drones, and that Mav and the others might be captured, or worse.

18

Betty marched into the cubicle with an authoritative stride and a grim aspect pinned to her face. The kind of face that someone puts on just to appear important.

Tel looked up as she stepped in.

"You are being summoned to a meeting," she announced with a look of impatience, as if Telanthia should have already divined the fact by her very presence.

"With whom?"

Betty's lips bunched up as if truly annoyed.

"You'll see. Now, get up and follow me!" she commanded.

Tel fell in step with her, stealing a nervous look at Rose and Camilla as she did.

Betty led her to a room where two WGs or Women's Guards stood in wait. One of them stepped toward Telanthia – flicking her hand. "Hold up your arms," at which she proceeded to do a thorough body-search. When she was done, the other opened the door, and with Tel sandwiched between them, they marched her to a waiting elevator, then to a vehicle which promptly whisked her off without a word spoken as to where or who she was meeting.

The car speared through the Manhattan streets and into a subterranean parking lot directly under the *One World Tower.*

Pressed between two more WGs – they escorted her in deathly silence, as if she were walking the green mile to her final execution. Stopping short of a set of double doors, she was directed inside an office, which although simplistic in design, was spacious and sprawling.

Standing at the far end, looking out the window at the New York skyline, was Lady V herself.

To anyone else, the moment would have been daunting, to be called into the presence of the President herself, but for Tel, it was different. In her mind, she was facing the enemy.

V turned, and in that briefest of brief moments, Tel caught the fleeting look in the woman's eyes; *was it fragility, or was it fear*, she wondered. One thing was certain, the arrogant demeanor that the President usually put up in public had been shaken by something, betrayed by the ripples of worry and anxiety that showed on her face.

Lady V approached with an asserted stride – as if every step were important in showing her unassailable power.

"Have a seat," she said with just a touch of authority while pointing to a chair.

V sat across from her, meticulously folding a leg over the other and clasping her fingers in her lap. It was then that Tel noticed the details of the woman's attire. Not only was she wearing her usual red leather tights, a body suit that seemed to have been poured over her frame, but her right hand and lower right arm were sheathed by a black leather strap, all of which was accentuated by long finger nails, blood-red in color, forged with meticulous care to add to an image of lethality.

"How are you enjoying your new life?" she asked with a supercilious tone, flagging that this was just preamble leading to the real agenda.

"It's okay, I'm adapting," lied Tel.

V smiled reservedly as they began a cat and mouse game.

"I'm told that you and your associates are working out well at Tetra-Drone."

"We like to think so."

"It's important to me that you succeed," said V, while standing and walking, once again, to the window, speaking without looking at Tel. It was a technique she enjoyed using, a means of throwing people off-balance.

"I'm curious," she continued, "now that you've had the opportunity to adapt, what do you think of New America?" She turned to register the reaction to her question.

Tel lightly shrugged. "It's different, I suppose," she answered, while assessing the waters.

"Different? How so?" asked V with a flick of her brow.

"It's not the world I'm accustomed to."

"You're referring to the fact that women dominate society, and men play only a minor role in it."

"That's a big part of it, yes."

The President moved nearer with her arms crossed over her chest. "Do you think it's wrong?"

"In some respects, I do."

"Men were a dying breed – what else would you have expected of us?" asked V as she closed the distance between them.

"I realize that, but they still have rights…"

V cut her off with a clip of her hand as if brandishing a sword. "Ah, human rights, is that the issue here?"

"If you insist on knowing my opinion…"

"I do."

"I think the *Inhumane Act* is a brilliant piece of work, and one that should have existed long ago - but as far as men go, it is a gross violation of their basic rights as human beings."

Lady V slipped back into the chair with her eyes locked on the other.

"Human rights." She huffed with a roll of her eyes. "I used to hear a lot of chatter and yack about that particular subject back before the *Cataclysm*, and yet, despite all the best efforts of many to protect our human rights, men still went ahead and started a war that killed millions and put us on the path to World War III."

"That was a singularity," replied Tel.

Lady V's head rocked back and forth with incredulity. "Really, a singularity?" Her tone shifted to near disgust as her voice rose in pitch. "Hundreds of wars have been fought by men over a matter of just a few centuries, I suppose those were singularities too.

Two world wars started by men in the space of just twenty-five years – wars that killed tens and tens of millions – another singularity? Or how about 15,000 plus nuclear warheads in the arsenals, just waiting to be launched against people, more singularities? Men committed nine out of ten murders in the world. Ninety-three percent of all prosecuted crimes - men." She paused. "Men are the common denominator behind all the shit in society."

"I am not challenging the facts. I am merely saying that taking away their rights is not the answer. And besides, men have also contributed to our advances."

V scoffed with a wave of her hand. "We're quite aware of their contributions to science, art, and the humanities; but in the end, what good is it if the net sum of their actions is the destruction of our race."

"Men didn't cause the *Cataclysm*."

"No, they did not; but they did nothing to prevent it from happening either. When they were warned of the threat, when they had the capability of doing so, when they could have used the nuclear arsenals for good instead of aggrandizing their egos and prancing on the global stage, they parked it aside as unimportant." She paused. "The guilt of omission is just as powerful as the guilt of commission. Shoot someone in the head and you are labelled a murderer; but stand by and do nothing while someone takes another's life, and mediocrity calls you a victim or an innocent bystander. I do not agree with that view. Men are complicit in both crimes against humanity because they insisted on holding onto the power, the means of destroying our world, and the means of protecting it from destruction, and they fucked up on both counts."

She stood, paced the room for a moment and then stopped to face Tel. "You're a scientist, do you think we could have stopped those rocks from hitting?"

"Possibly," she nodded.

V raised a finger to the air. "Of course, we could have. In fact, the records show that NASA and even ESA, had designed orbiting stations between Mars and the asteroid belt, which could have detected potentially dangerous rocks well in advance, and disrupted their flight paths long before they became a threat to us. Why didn't they get built?" She raised a brow. "It is simple! War is profit – it always has been. The rich get richer by it. Corporations got bigger. Bankers profited from the plunder and the real estate they scooped up from the dead. The military arena, in the age of men, was one of the largest industries in the world and men in power were not about to forsake it – certainly not to build an orbital defense system to ensure that our race survived." She grinned. "And yet, here we are today, women are in control, and look what happens, we abolish the war machines, we ditch all the weapons of mass destruction, and we focus on profiting from peace and prosperity - and not death."

"You didn't call me here to discuss the virtues of your new utopia, so, why am I here?"

The President resumed her seat. "I want to know about Tanner McNeal."

And there it was! "What do you want to know?"

"You spent sixteen years with the man, confined to a small ship and the HAB, and two years in preparation for the mission, what's he like?"

"He was a good man and great captain."

"A modest response."

Tel tipped her head at the woman. "You have access to his NASA profile. Why ask me?"

"I have read everything I could find out about him but even the ship's log provides little insight about the man himself. I know that you and the rest of the crew survived touchy situations along the way. Life on Europa was not easy, was it?"

"No, it was a constant vigil," answered Tel, watching the eyes of the woman. *She was fishing for something, but what*, she wondered.

"Were you close to him?" probed V.

Tel felt a nervous shudder. "As close as anyone."

V circled her, like a lion, and finally stopped behind her. "I saw something in Tanner McNeal's eyes when we first met. Every time your name came up in our discussions, the nuances of his body language changed." She lingered.

"What do you mean?"

V grinned as she circled back in front. "Call it woman's intuition, but I got the distinct impression that you two were more than just work mates.

Tel shook her head, trying to disguise her growing concern and not wanting to say or do anything that could compromise Tanner. "There were strict mandates from NASA about inter-crew relations. It was off the table."

V raised a brow, her eyes revealing her suspicion. "You didn't answer my question."

"What exactly is it that you want to know from me?" asked Tel, her patience thinning.

The President cocked her head to one side as her brows furrowed. "I want to know what makes him tick."

"Why not ask him, you locked him away," her brash and unrestrained answer evoked a stern look from the President who stepped even closer.

"You don't like me, do you?"

The wall of social propriety between them suddenly vanished, like smoke in the wind.

"I don't like people who abuse others in the name of any agenda?"

"You still think, after everything I just said, that I'm abusing human rights?"

"You've reduced men to a worker-slave class, I'd call that a violation of their inherent rights."

V's eyes narrowed. "Considering the circumstances, I would call that a childish mentality. Do you really think that my perspective on this is unique?" Her brow furrowed. "You think those women out there would ever trust a man with power again? You think the leaders and people of other nations would ever give men the power to do it all over again?" She shook her head. "You do not seem to appreciate what we went through to put this society back together again as a decent, crime-free world, where women can truly be women and where the sky is the limit. Why do you fight it?"

"If you are talking to me purely as a woman, the paradigm has virtues. But…" she paused, fixing her gaze on V, "… we are not just women, we are human beings, and moreover, souls of a higher order. And while I acknowledge what has been accomplished after the *Cataclysm*, your perfect society just does not fit into my moral compass."

Lady V guffawed, a loud, brassy, and bellowing sound, more like a cloaked scream than humor. "My god, you really are a product of the epoch you come from."

Tel decided to play her ace card. "I assume Tanner escaped, is that why you want to know more about him?"

V waited in silence.

"Let me tell you about the man you seemed so concerned about. Tanner is a man of principle," she began. “The entire crew owe their lives to him. I have seen him step outside the HAB without a full suit on, putting himself in mortal jeopardy, to save three of his crew from imminent death, and he nearly lost his fingers to the freezing cold of Europa. His impulse is always to think about others first.” She looked up at V who listened intently. “He’s a fighter and if he has escaped, he won’t give up until he accomplishes his goal.”

“And what goal is that?”

Tel tipped her head to one side, pausing to think a moment, “I think Tanner is coming after you.”

“And you think I or my regime are vulnerable to a handful of men, men who are probably at this very moment feeling the effects of the virus which permeates their bodies, and without the vaccine, who will most certainly perish in due time?” retorted V with a smug look. “Tanner is no threat to me. I will play the clock – because I have time, and he does not.”

19

“If we stay north-west, following that star,” pointed Matis at the star-speckled sky, “we should hit Freeport soon enough.”

Michael Brenner grinned before speaking. “Yeah, and once we’re there it’s Bonnie and Clyde all over again, right?”

Mav raised a brow, thinking to himself that Brenner, despite the intended joke, was right. They had been reduced to thieves, stealing what they needed to survive.

After a time, they crested a hill and looked down on the small sleepy town of Freeport, Pennsylvania. Streetlights created a patchwork of light and dark, while a dull October moon added to the somnolent ambience that held the town in its embrace.

Mav pulled out the military binoculars and scanned the streets until he found a grocery store that was within easy reach. Within ten minutes they had managed to jimmy the back door and were inside.

"Focus on canned goods, not perishables," said Mav as he grabbed a large plastic bag from the cashier's counter and started piling stuff into it. In a matter of minutes, they had bags heavily laden with goods.

As they exited, Brenner caught sight of something shimmering in the air above. "Fuck!" he pointed upward as the drone swooped in, its scanner casting a blue light over their faces.

Mav instantly dropped his bags, pulled the Glock from his waist band, and fired three rounds at the robotic, one of which smashed into its ocular dome. A mechanical squeal emitted and filled the air as it fell and crashed into the asphalt - shattering into a dozen pieces.

They charged back in the direction from which they came, but the damage was already done. The gunshots had woken the whole town. Darkened houses were suddenly lighting up like dominoes as people peered out their windows and doorways. It was not long before calls were received by *CAB*, the *Central Assessment Bureau,* and within minutes, Lady V was roused from her sleep by a Visio wavering in the air above her bed.

"Ma'am," said her secretary with a tenuous voice, wanting to wake the leader but not annoy her.

V cracked an eye. "What is it?"

"Calls were just received from Freeport, PA. Men were spotted running away. A drone was shot down outside a food store."

Lady V grinned as she slipped from the bed and walked toward the bathroom, speaking as she did.

"Deploy more drones – I want them ready to act on my order."

"Yes, Ma'am."

20

The three stumbled through the opening of the cave, their bags spilling out as they did. Their faces reflected the desperate race they had just endured.

Mav dropped to the ground, as did the others, heaving and gasping for his next breath as sweat poured off him. He looked up at Tanner, his words coming between fragmented gulps.

"A drone…" he gasped. "It spotted us before I shot it down."

"Okay. Drink and eat, and then get ready to move," announced Tanner, then turning to the others who now clustered nearby to find out what was going on.

One large man emerged from the group.

"What's the plan?" he asked with a sonorous voice.

"What's your name?" asked Tanner.

"Cal Williams," answered the large man, his body chiseled by years of chipping and hauling coal from the mines.

"We can't outrun them at this point, Cal, especially with their condition," he nodded toward the group nearby.

Cal stepped even closer, speaking in a hushed voice. "Look, most of those guys are wasted. They will not survive a hard run or even a fight at this point. There are a few of us who are prepared to split hairs," he paused as his face was molded by a grim determination. "We want in. Give us weapons." He lingered. "We'd rather die fighting than rotting in that hellhole again."

21

From the small breakfast nook of her apartment in Brooklyn, Tel watched as the sun began its final dance on the distant stage, where the sky and the Earth meet in an explosion of shimmering colors; hues of red and pink and orange that glimmered and flickered like the waning light of an expiring candle.

As the last tendrils of the sun's ambassadors splashed against the clouds – announcing the sun's final departure, she let the conversation, earlier that day with the President, play over and over, in her head.

Tanner was a real concern to V, and now that she had openly expressed her disaffection toward the woman, it was just a matter of time before she would come under attack too.

She had studied enough sociopathic case histories during her training as a behavioral specialist to understood what drove their paranoia and the depth of their empathy-less world; and the compulsions that made them do things, criminal things, in the name of self-preservation. Lady V, despite her attempts to appear otherwise, showed obvious signs of a sociopathic persona. She was obsessed with her own monolithic image and the ideological waves which drove her ship; and clearly, she would do anything in her power to ensure that her position was never challenged.

As she watched the dark hand of night consume the land, it suddenly occurred to her that Lady V might well resort to another stratagem.

A familiar rap sounded on her door.

It is open, Camilla."

The Argentinian quietly slipped into the one-room apartment.

Camilla was a slim woman, with milk-chocolate skin, intensely dark hair and deeply set eyes, the whole exotic package – and yet a demure creature, one who never flaunted her physical attributes, being more interested in her intellectual prowess than her sexual merits.

She was, amongst all her talents, the most brilliant IT technician that Tel had ever met, and for that matter, her special skill set was the main reason that NASA had selected her for the mission to Jupiter. While her knowledge as a microbiologist and in bioengineering were impressive, ironically, it was her early history as a hacker that had really earned her a spot on the mission. NASA wanted someone aboard the *Dauntless* who could, in the event of any unforeseen circumstances, thread a digital needle through the smallest and most complex of cybernetic holes and could navigate their way through problems that might arise. The very lifeline of the crew depended on the functionality of its holistic digital mind. And on more than one occasion, Camilla had easily slipped into that role and had fixed potentially catastrophic breakdowns in life support, navigational and other critical systems.

Tel tipped her head at a bottle of Merlot on the table. “Help yourself, girl.”

No sooner had Camilla poured herself a glass when the door opened and the brash Welsher, Rose, pounded her way into the room like a water Buffalo, eyed Tel with a tight lip, poured herself a glass of Merlot without even asking, and then downed it in one gulp.

She dropped into the seat next to Camilla and turned an eye to Tel. “So, tell me, why did that scrubber want to see you?”

“She wanted to know about Tanner.”

Camilla’s head bobbed gently as she let out a sigh. “So, it is Tanner behind all of this commotion.”

“Oh yeah,” smiled Tel. “Our boy has created a shitstorm in Oz, and the Wizard herself is spooked.”

“Does she know about you two?” asked Rose with a grin. “You know, the side you guys tried to hide rather unsuccessfully?” her grin widened.

“I do not know. She is a tricky bitch. I tried not to show anything, but you know me, I wear my feelings on my sleeve.”

Rose grinned at her, “And, you’re a lousy actor too, especially when it comes to Tanner.”

“Anyhow,” continued Tel, “I’m worried that V is planning to use us as leverage to get to him.”

“What do you mean?” asked Rose.

"If she threatens us, Tanner might take the bait."

22

As dawn announced itself with a flourish of light charging into the darkened world, the taciturn ambience of their surroundings was transformed to something surreal, nightmarish in fact, as a wall of drones hung in the air, like a legion of soldiers, hovering in front of the cave entrance.

Beyond them was a squad of thirty or so *WGs*, *Women's Guards* – with their weapons aimed up at them.

Tanner stared through the opening, with Mav and others, as the grim-faced women looked back at them – their faces as hard and hateful as ice. What really sent a chill down their backs were the one-eyed robots, silently poised, like a swarm of killer bees, each one of them capable of killing multiple men in just seconds.

"They're not making a move, why?" hushed Mav.

Tanner's face reflected his dread. "I'll wager that V doesn't want to draw first blood – she's waiting for us to throw the first punch."

Just then, a drone broke from the swarm and moved silently toward Tanner, its ocular dome fixed on him as the indigo light fanned his face and his alone.

A Visio projected from the drone with the face of Lady V, as if she were standing right there.

A perverse smile crept across her lips. "Hello Tanner. By now it must be obvious that you cannot escape me." Her eyes casually drifted to the other men who stood around him, looking at each with utter disdain, and then back to him. "Trying to do so is futile at this point and would just result in a fight that you cannot win."

Tanner raised a brow. "How far are you willing to go with this, V? Because, from where I am standing, we are prepared to fight it out to the death."

"Silly boys and their silly weapons," she huffed with a derisive chuckle. "You men never change, do you? Each of those drones carry enough pellets to take out a dozen men. Do you really want to see how effective they are?"

"You'd like that, wouldn't you, a photo-op and a chance to criminalize us on national television?"

"Say what you will, but the cave you find yourselves huddled inside, like rats, will not protect you." She paused. "I will give you fifteen minutes, which is more than you deserve. Talk it over with your men. If you choose not to surrender, I will resort to using force."

The projection vanished as the drone slipped away from the cave and resumed its spot in line with the others.

Tanner moved back inside the cave and hunkered down with the others. Cal Williams dropped next to him.

"Surrender is out of the question," exclaimed Michael with an angry flourish of his hand. "If she wants a fight, I'll happily give it to her," he said, gripping his weapon.

Tanner sighed. "Let us not go there yet. Besides, think about those men over there," said Tanner. "They won't survive a fight – not in their condition."

Michael's verve deflated.

"Come on, guys, we've survived all the shit that Europa threw at us and more – we need an idea and fast."

After a moment of silence, Petar chimed in. "I've got one," he said with a devilish grin and proceeded to lay it out for them.

"Vote?" asked Tanner.

"Sounds good to me," said Mav.

"I say yes," added Brenner and the others also silently nodded their assent.

23

Tel peered down the dark street.

It was well before dawn, and apart from a handful of passing cars and passersby's, the byways of the city were devoid of prying eyes.

Behind her, Rose and Camilla huddled close to the wall.

Like her, they had changed into dark pants, hoodies, and a jacket, making them less conspicuous – at least they hoped that was the case, because with the drones and the surveillance network of cameras which existed in the new "utopia" – privacy was a luxury, not a God-given right.

The plan had been forged in the wake of two empty bottles of wine – and whether the alcohol had catalyzed their decision, or not, they had come to the same conclusion – it was time to leave before Lady V scooped them up and used them as pawns in her sick game.

Now, with nightfall as their main ally, they worked their way along the quiet streets, block by block. The plan was simple enough; get to the station, take a train to the far reaches of Long Island, to Sag Harbor at the furthest tip, in the hopes that an old friend, Linda Ross, was still alive, one Tel had known from her teenage years.

As plans go, it had plenty of holes; such as getting on the train without the security cameras betraying them; or, for that matter, arriving to the house she so well-remembered from her youth, and where she had spent several summers with her best friend at the time, only to find that maybe Linda had perished in the aftermath of the *Cataclysm*, or she no longer lived there, or worse-case scenario, that her teenage friend was now drinking Lady V's brand of Kool Aid and would instantly turn them in. But something inside her said otherwise, and she hoped that her feelings were not simply pandering false hope – because once they were found missing, she knew that Lady V would initiate a full-scale search for them.

For an hour, they slipped from one dark recess to another, waiting for streets to clear of late-night traffic, or people, and then they would dart to the next corner, pause, and then continue, following a path that eventually took them within sight of the train station.

"We go separately, not as a threesome," whispered Tel. "Keep your head low, do not look up anytime, and sit facing away from cameras. Get off at the Bridgehampton stop. I will be waiting across the street."

Tel made it aboard the train without incident. The ride, however, was nerve-racking, and certainly not the anticipation of pleasure and excitement which she so vividly recalled experiencing when had taken this very train to visit her friend a lifetime ago. Now, every stop, and every new person boarding, sent a wave of fear streaking through her. It was not only new eyes, but it was also the possibility that a WG would step aboard, or worse, the one-eyed beast, a drone.

As she stepped from the train at Bridgehampton, a brutally cold October wind slapped her in the face. The North Atlantic gust carried the scent of salt and fish, one that instantly exhumed old memories she had of walking these very beaches, playing in the ocean with her friend, eating double-dipped ice cream cones, all the while utterly oblivious to anything in the world except her all-encompassing happiness at the time.

Pulling the hoodie tight over her head to evade the shrill bite that swirled around her, Tel remained vigilant to the fact that cameras located around the station were the eyes of Lady V – who could be watching her this very moment.

As she looked about, anxiously awaiting the next train to arrive in thirty minutes, she sighed, thinking to herself that Europa had been a paradise compared to Earth.

24

In the precious minutes left, Mav, and the others, along with the whole troop of bedraggled souls, silently slipped into the depths of the cavern, following in the footsteps of Dep who had disappeared hours before. The fact that Dep had not shown back up, either meant he had found a way out, or was still going. In either case, the option was better than a suicidal show-down with the drones.

Tanner held back with Petar.

Patience was not a virtue of Lady V's, and precisely on the fifteen-minute mark, the drone once again moved and stopped in front of Tanner's face. He stiffened, feeling a knot forming in the pit of his stomach as sweat now beaded over his body.

The Visio appeared.

"So, Captain, what's your decision?" asked V with a cavalier taunt in her voice – as if she were giving him a minute of her precious time.

"Before I answer that question, what will you do to us if we do surrender?"

"The men you broke out will be returned to the camps."

"And my men?"

She paused, a deceptive moment where she tried to hide her true intent, but somehow, Tanner divined her mendacity.

"I cannot guarantee your fate, McNeal, but I can assure you that those poor bastards you broke out will get a chance to live another day. And as we both know, if they do not get their injections soon, they will die, as will you and your men."

"Your hypocrisy really has no bounds, does it?" he said.

Her eyes narrowed with anger in them, like dark trenches in a field. "You have balls, McNeal. I could have sent my drones in there and wiped out every one of you, to a man, without my WG having to move an inch. You do not get to make any deals here if that is what you are thinking?"

"So, everyone goes back to the camps and works until they die, and my men and myself, we get to face the music – is that it?"

She shrugged. "You started this fight, not me. You and your men knew the consequences when you set off on this path."

"You took away our rights and put us in a prison. Did you really expect us to lie down and submit, like acquiescent little slaves at your behest?"

A shroud of distemper clouded her face as she shook her head. "Those are the rules of engagement – rules you obviously refuse to abide by."

Tanner studied her face, an unflinching and joyless one that watched him with ruthless eyes. "You like to think that you're better than us, don't you?" he said.

She canted her head. "I don't think that at all, Tanner, I know I'm better than you."

At that point, all he was trying to accomplish was stalling for Petar. He could see him in his peripheral vision as the man's hands moved rapidly.

He stepped closer, looking her in the eyes, "You've been drinking too much of your own Kool Aid, V, you've lost your perspective."

She laughed – a raucous grating sound. Then she fixed a glare on him. "You like to think that, make me out as the bad guy just because you are at the disadvantage here, but I assure you Tanner McNeal, my perspective has never been clearer. Now…" she flicked her hand at him dismissively, "… this discourse is accomplishing nothing. I need your decision." she commanded with an imperious tone.

Petar suddenly gave him the thumbs up. Tanner looked her in the face with a smile on his lips. "The answer is no."

"So, you refuse to surrender?"

"To the last man."

Her lips tightened as her jaws clenched. "Then you leave me no choice," she said as her image faded. The drone receded back in line with the others.

Tanner instantly dropped back and crouched behind a large boulder, with Petar next to him.

"Cover your ears, Cap – this could hurt," he said with a surreptitious grin.

The drones charged, sweeping in toward the cave, and as they did, the blast ripped a hole in the air, a violent and pounding concussion that knocked them on their backs as the C4 explosive, which Petar had casually pocketed during their raid of the armory, lit up the cave.

A deep rumbling echoed throughout the cavern, resonating off the walls, like the guttural roar of an unearthly beast rising from hell itself; while a literal avalanche of stone cascaded around the front of the cave, and a choking cloud of dust billowed outward like the sands of a desert storm.

As they coughed up the pasty film which layered their throats, Petar wiped his eyes and peered into the diminishing haze. "Fuck me, that was cool," he said with a large grin.

Cautiously they stood and approached the heap of rocks which now blocked the cave entrance, their weapons aimed into the rubble in search of any holes or signs of drones that might have made it through.

Satisfied that they were safe, at least for now, they turned away, but a scratching sound caught their attention. Both spun in unison, following the noise until they saw it, a singular drone was trapped beneath a large slab of rock. It twisted and squirmed to free itself, like an animal desperately clawing to escape the maws of inevitable death.

Its dome swiveled up to look at the two men as they peered down at it. Tanner wanted Lady V to see his face. He flipped a finger for her to see and then placed the nozzle of his gun into its dome and fired off two rounds, killing it dead.

25

The echo of scraping and the heavy trod of feet, along with the subtle murmurings of men's voices, gently echoed back through the rocky passage, a sign that somewhere up ahead of them, Mav and the others were negotiating their way through the bowels of this underworld.

Time and distance were deceptive inside the bowels of the Earth. There were no markers, no sun or sky or other signs to tell them how far they had gone, whether they were heading east or west or simply going in circles. There was just endless rock, the choking and foreboding walls, narrow passages, and meager crawl spaces, which could easily crush them or pin them in this tomb forever.

At times, noises carried well, encouraging sounds that they were on the right track; while in other parts it seemed as if they were lost in the gloomy doom of a subterranean world.

A silent voice echoed in Tanner's head as he clawed his way through a narrow passage – barely wide enough for his body. It was the voice of endless silence, the one he had met in space, while standing on that precipice on Europa. It was the same sound he sensed when he speared the skies as a test pilot, and the same one that he felt as a young boy, locked in a room without food. Silence was his therapy, because it touched him at the core of his soul, calming him and helping him to see his way through the machinations and complexities of humanity.

"Fucking rocks!" exclaimed Petar as he cut his hand again. "I will never go into a cave, not ever again," he redoubled his affirmation.

The flashlight in Tanner's hand cast long, phantom-like shadows, which bounced off the walls ahead, foreboding visions of strange underworld creatures that lurked and waited for them.

He wondered about Dep. "You think he found a way out?" he whispered.

"Who, Dep?"

Tanner nodded.

"He's a wily little fuck," answered the Serb with a smirk. "Remember, on Europa, when he rigged that explosive to make a hole in the ice, so we could run our tests in the sub-strata?"

Tanner grinned, wiping sweat from his dirt-caked face as he did. "How can I forget. It rained ice for an hour."

"Yeah, that was fun."

The comment was distractive, but it reminded him of the moment when Tel and Camilla ecstatically announced that that they had found a sub-order of virus, ten meters down, where it was warmer than on the surface of Europa. It was one of the high points of their entire mission, the first discovery of another bio-form, and proof that life existed elsewhere within our very solar system.

That discovery was trumped later, however, when they discovered *Footprint*, something that had not yet become exposed – and might never if Lady V had her way.

26

Three lone figures trudged along the gravely shoulder of Sagg Road, a less-used estuary than the main trunk between Sag Harbor and Bridgehampton.

The sting of a brisk autumn wind scratched at their exposed skin, and the bite of their hungry stomachs growled like ravenous wolves - reminding them that they had not eaten since the day before.

"Bloody hell, girl," began Rose over the din of a ceaseless wind, "couldn't you have picked the Bahamas, somewhere warm."

Tel smiled, reminded that Rose, while a brilliant scientist, had another side to her, one that could unleash a torrent of distempered profanity when she wanted to.

"We're nearly there, Rose, relax."

When they finally reached the outskirts of the quaint town of Sag Harbor, Tel pointed, "It's up ahead," she said, now anxious to get off the streets before anyone saw them, and even more anxious to know if her gamble had paid off or if she had just sunk them deeper into the mud.

The house that Tel was looking for suddenly loomed.

Unlike the other homes, its lawn had been taken over by tall grass and weeds, the bushes were unkempt and the grove of trees to one side, once proud and strapping, now hung like old, withered men, their boughs weighed down by more than just age.

What she remembered of it, the images she had so fondly stashed away in her happy place, was that of a pastoral painting, like a Rembrandt, an inviting and cheerful home, painted in canary yellow with a brilliant white banister girding its front porch.

She stood there, momentarily transfixed by the startling dilapidated imposter –its façade no longer fresh and bright, instead, its paint was peeling off like skin inflicted with leprosy; and the white banister that once girded the front, its true hallmark, now leaned and wobbled like an old woman, broken in several places – appearing more like the relic of a war-torn survivor, than the warm inviting home she remembered.

Oh god, she thought, *maybe I was wrong to come here.*

Rose stepped up beside her and pointed. “That piece of shit is where your friend lives?”

Tel sighed. “Wait here.”

Approaching the house with both caution and trepidation reining her in, she searched for any signs of life within. A light, or other movement, but there was nothing to see through the shuttered windows.

Her heart and her hopes began to sink.

As her foot touched the porch, she was met by the sound of creaking boards, the sort of moan that betrayed both neglect and antiquity.

For a moment she hung there, her mind filled with growing anxiety. *If Linda was not here, where else could we go,* she thought.

The image of her old friend and all the memories she cherished, now poured in, like warm light touching her soul. She sensed the echo of their laughter, the pitch of Linda's voice as they spoke about their dreams, their flirtations, and their plans to conquer the world.

A longing sigh breeched her lips, and then, with a quick glance back at the worried faces of her two friends, Tel closed the doors to that past, forcing herself to concentrate on the task at hand.

Stepping forward, the boards responded with another chorus of creaks.

She knocked on the door.

Silence ensued – only the sound of the wind rustling in the nearby trees met her ears.

Once again, she knocked. This time a faint stirring echoed from within, as if someone was moving, slowly and hesitantly, shuffling ever closer.

As the door creaked open, she was met by the inquiring face of an older-looking woman, with wisps of gray in her thinning hair and a wrinkled visage. Her frail body was angled to one side, heavily supported by a cane in one hand.

She shuffled forward, closing the distance between them as her eyes grew wider.

When she spoke, the voice was unmistakable. "Tel?"

27

The funnel of light from the flashlight he held suddenly revealed a fork in the tunnel ahead.

"Shit!" he swore with a hushed voice. Tanner approached the one to the left, pressing an ear to the passage to see if he could hear any sounds echoing back, and then he repeated the same with the other.

Petar mimicked his action, then looked up at Tanner with a shake of his head. "I don't hear anything, Cap."

With an ever-present and growing anxiety that drones might soon catch up with them, Tanner made a snap decision. "Wait here, I'll go down this one and see where it goes."

"And if you don't come back?"

"Then you take the other one and hook up with Mav."

Petar wagged his head defiantly. "Nope, I'll wait here for you to come back or I'm coming after you."

"I could pull rank on you right now."

"A pointless exercise," grinned the Serb.

Tanner drew a deep breath and then slipped into the dark passage, once again surrounded by a mountain of rock pressing in from all sides. An exasperated rasp exited his throat as he dreamed of fresh air and the open sky. Right now, he would do anything to be free of this tomb.

Like a drunken sailor, swaying this way and that, up and down, like the flop of a boat caught in the grip of an ocean storm, the tunnel weaved ahead.

Once again, he felt that haunting sensation, the one that had tormented him aboard the *Dauntless* - claustrophobia.

Of course, the obvious question was why go into space if one hated being pressed into a box, because the life of an astronaut was tantamount to living inside a tin can. But logic aside, passion had driven him to overcome his fear – and once again, passion was all he had now to keep his mind off the overwhelming sense of being swallowed alive.

Suddenly, the narrow passage washed out into an open and dark cavern.

Tanner felt relieved. He could finally stand upright.

He stretched his sore back, while casting his flashlight against the walls. Its beam revealed a cathedral of spiraling rock columns that ended in a solid ceiling high above – but there was no sign of an opening, and certainly, no sign of Mav and the legion of men who had followed him.

Fuck! he exclaimed, dread creeping over him at the thought of having to retrace his steps.

A grating sound broke the taciturnity, a mere scraping, but here in the tomb, it was like having someone shouting in his ear.

Tanner gripped his gun and spun to meet it, and there, standing not a meter away, was Dep - blood dripping from his forehead.

28

The three women sat quietly on the sofa waiting patiently as anxiety played havoc on their nerves, feeling, in an odd way, as if they had just tumbled down a very deep rabbit hole and had lost touch with reality altogether.

For Tel, the moment was beyond surreal.

Shock had set in the instant when she realized she was looking at her old friend, Linda Ross, the same blue eyes, the same smile, and yet, one now embraced by a sea of sagging and sickly pale skin, none of which made any sense to her.

Moreover, the house inside defied every image she had stored away in the vaults of her past, memories of her days spent here as a young teen on the threshold of womanhood.

A musty scent dominated, the smell of a forgotten place, an old place – even impending death, while dust could be seen layering the furnishings and lamps.

Tel stole a glance at Linda as she stooped over

the counter in the kitchen, preparing them food.

Sadness began to fill her heart as she watched her shuffling, slowly and painfully. Finally, Linda hobbled toward them with the help of her cane, balancing a small tray in the other hand. Tel rose to help her, but she shook her head. "Nope!" she announced vociferously. "I can manage this, Tel," her eyes were firm with determination, like a war veteran who refused to be treated like an invalid.

Sliced cake and hot cups of coffee taunted their hungry bodies as Linda eased herself into an armchair across from them, her pain written on her face as she did.

She looked up at them and raised a brow.

"Well, what are you waiting for – eat up!"

After devouring the cake and draining their coffee cups, Linda was satisfied she had performed her due diligence and broke the silence. She smiled at Tel.

"How have you been, my friend?"

Tel lowered her coffee cup to the table, reticent to speak her mind. "I've seen better days, but…" she paused.

"But what?"

"It's just that …" she hesitated.

Linda cut her off with a flick of her hand as if reading Tel's mind.

"If you are worried that I am going turn you girls in, you can put your minds at rest. I don't drink V's brand of bullshit."

Relief washed over the three, like a storm suddenly passing.

"So …" she began with an expectant look on her face, "What brings you three to Sag Harbor, the center of nowhere?"

Over the course of the next hour, they told Linda everything, from their mission to Europa, to the unfolding episodes back on Earth.

When they were done, Linda stood without saying a word and shuffled to the kitchen, where she promptly made a fresh pot of coffee and then returned with it and even more cakes.

"Now," she began, "… how can I help?"

"Can we stay here for a while? I know it is asking a lot, but we need to be off the radar until I can figure out our next step," asked Tel.

"Of course, you can."

Now it was Tel's turn to inquire. "What happened to you, Linda?"

The woman shrugged with a dismissive flick of her brows. "Oh, you mean this piece of shit," she cast a deprecating look at her withered hands. "It's a bit of a shocker, I know, not exactly what you expected to see when I opened the door, right?"

Her eyes betrayed her shame despite her attempt to marginalize it. "After you rocketed off to Jupiter, I decided to jump the pond and went to Japan to train on medical techniques I wanted to learn for my own career. Unfortunately," she lingered. "I was there when the nukes hit North Korea."

"You got dosed with radiation?" asked Rose.

"More than a dose, honey. The prevailing winds carried the radioactive cloud right over Sendai, in the north, where I was working, – barely three hundred kilometers from ground zero where eight nukes hit the coastal region of North Korea."

"We heard it was four," said Camilla.

Linda huffed unglamorously. "You got the redacted version. That douchebag of a President of ours did not have the balls to admit that he had just murdered close to twenty million people, so he made sure that a more palatable story was released." She chuckled. "And of course, he accused the press of being fake news – what irony, uh!?"

"He was a fucking wanker," said Rose.

"Indeed, he was. Anyhow, the fall-out was massive and it caused panic in Japan. Remember, they are the only people up until that time who had nukes dropped on them." She paused, reflective. "I got out of there two weeks later, but by then, the winds had already dropped enough radiation on Japan to light it up like a neon tube." She touched her lips to her coffee cup and sipped gingerly on the hot brew. "When I got back to the States the symptoms were already there and doctors told me I had a year or two, at best."

"How did you survive this long," asked Tel with saddened eyes.

Linda shrugged. "Luck or the fact that I am a stubborn bitch and refuse to give up. In truth, the medicos had a tough time diagnosing my condition. The abridged version is that my exposure to repeated waves of radiation catalyzed a degenerative disease in me. Instead of regenerating cells, which the body naturally does, I have been dying ahead of my years as my body systematically shut down. What you see is the withering remains of your memories of that bright-eyed red head with the perky tits."

Tel squeezed Linda's hand.

"How long do you have?" asked Camilla.

"I'm on the homerun, honey - maybe six months before my ticket expires."

"I'm so sorry," said Tel, as tears pooled in her eyes.

Linda touched her hand to Tel's, "Oh, my dearest friend, you have nothing to apologize for. I do not feel sorry for myself, so don't you start with that maudlin crap. I want you to remember me as that snappy seventeen-year-old who used to steal my dad's beer and smoke weed with you out in the back shed."

Tel forced a quivering smile to her lips as she wiped her tears away.

Rose interceded in the silence that followed. "Tell me, since you've survived two worlds, the one before and after the *Cataclysm*, why is everyone acting like a nutter?"

Linda raised a finger to the air – addressing them now like a teacher in a class.

"That seed was planted a long time ago, Rose, when men built and stockpiled nuclear weapons under the delusion that they would only exist as a preventative measure." She paused. "But, if you're referring to the current utopia, you're missing the bigger picture."

"But do you agree with any of this?" probed Rose obstinately.

Linda shrugged as a small grin crept onto her lips. "I am a woman, like you, like all those women out there, and admittedly, it is wonderful that we no longer have to battle and fight for our relevance in a man's world anymore. But I am no man-hater."

For a time, she was silent, her eyes flicking back, and forth as old visions taunted her to walk down dark roads, the memories she had long ago stuffed in closets.

"When you assume that everyone has gone mad, you are being terribly arrogant and very dismissive about what we had to endure," she leveled a hard look at Rose. "The magnitude of pain, suffering and death from those nukes and then the rocks hitting us, was transformative on an individual, collective, cultural, and global scale unlike anything that humanity has ever experienced. You did not live through the agony of seeing family and friends perish, watching as the society around you fell to pieces, as mountains of dead bodies piled up at burn sites. Imagine your worst horror film and multiply that by a hundred and you might come close to matching that reality we faced. I cannot even begin to describe the sheer magnitude of it. I do not think the stench of death will ever leave me."

Linda winced, ever so slightly as the pain and suffering touched her again from a dark place within.

"Admittedly, they are slurping up V's bullshit, but in a way, can you really blame them?" She raised a brow. "No one wanted to live through such a trauma ever again. So, when the dust settled, and men started dying in droves, we knew that our time had come." She looked Rose in the eyes – a hard look. "It is not madness you see, Rose. Even if they seem fanatical, zealous, or acquiescent, it is not a fair judgement of them. They felt betrayed by the men who were entrusted with power. And yes," she cast a hand to the air, "there were women to blame too for the shit that went down, our hands were not entirely clean; but, there is no question in anyone's mind that the balance of power resided in men's hands: and if you had survived what they endured, you might be embracing this new paradigm with enthusiasm as opposed to disgust."

Rose remained defiantly silent.

"How did V come to be the President?" asked Camilla.

"V hit the streets after the dust settled and started organizing women under the banner of WIP."

"You mean, *Women in Power*?" said Rose.

Linda nodded. "Obviously, she had an agenda, one fueled by more than just the *Cataclysm* itself, which she used to fan the flames for radical change. And given the circumstances, the trauma, the pain, the titanic level of destruction, her movement easily became the great white hope, and she used that zeitgeist to band women together and to empower them. She quickly became recognized as an iconic figure, at least here in America."

Linda pointed to an old time-worn globe sitting on a nearby counter. "The paradigm is not identical everywhere you go today, but the basic mentality is. For instance, if you go to Scandinavia, you will find a more progressive attitude and more leniency toward men than here in America. Same in Germany, or Argentina or Canada, the more moderate-minded nations. But if you go to the Middle East, Egypt, Syria, Saudi Arabia, Iran, and the like, where religious ideology and fervor had previously dictated the relative rights of women, you will find a culture which has morphed into a much more radical one than here."

Linda chuckled. "Those gals over there were really upset and when they got the chance, they seized control, and they are not about to relinquish it to men – not ever. Anyhow," she waved a cavalier hand to the air, "you wanted to know why women today are drinking V's Kool Aid, well, there's your answer."

Silence followed until Linda broke it with her next comment. "You girls are in a very precarious situation right now – you know that, right?"

"Any suggestions?" asked Tel.

"In fact, I do. Join up with the Resistance."

29

Dep slumped to the ground.

Tanner's flashlight revealed streaks of dirt and sweat, coursed with fresh blood which had splashed over one side of Dep's face. Heavy breaths exuded as his chest heaved from exertion.

"I found an exit," he said, breathing hard and fast, "but they were waiting there for us."

"The WG?"

Dep responded with a despondent nod. "The other two men were captured or killed – not sure. I managed to get away but not before hitting my head on the edge of a rock," he said, gingerly touching a finger to the nasty gash.

"How far back are they?"

"Maybe four or five hundred meters."

"Any drones?"

Dep nodded.

"Shit!" Tanner gritted his teeth as he helped Dep to his feet. "Keep up with me," he said as he turned back in the direction he had come, and together they ran through the twisting rocky passage. Behind them they could hear the high pitch of a woman's voice. A clear sign that the WG were closing in.

It seemed to take forever, but finally, they stumbled through the opening.

Petar jumped to his feet. "What the fuck!" he exclaimed, seeing the blood caked on Dep's face and the panic in Tanner's eyes.

"No time to explain," said Tanner as he picked up one of the grenade launchers they had pilfered from the armory. "You two get out of here. I'll be right behind you."

As the two men disappeared down the other tunnel, Tanner crouched in front of the passage, and listened as the sound of approaching guards grew more audible.

He aimed the launcher up into the rock ceiling above the opening.

Just then a drone swept around the corner, hovered momentarily, and then charged right at him.

Tanner squeezed the trigger.

30

Frustrating as it was to be denied her prize, Lady V was, in her own perverse way, enjoying the chase, particularly in the knowledge that Tanner and his men were now trapped inside a mountain, and she had her WG and drones watching every point of egress. It was just a matter of time, a cat and mouse game, before they were caught, or eventually expired somewhere deep in the mountainous tomb.

Her next task, both to capitalize on the event and to allay any concerns among her loyal following, since lips are loose, and people do talk, was to frame the incident within the parameters of her own agenda.

Since she exerted tremendous control over the media, and given the incubated nature of her nation, it was easy to impress perceptions as opposed to truth, on the minds of millions.

That very afternoon she appeared on national television with a live broadcast from her office in The Center.

"Word may have reached your ears that a small group of men escaped from a mining facility near Pittsburgh. These men, as men do, broke into an armory, stole weapons, and then promptly ambushed a convoy of trucks and released more men. The Women's Guard and our advanced DRC, the ***D****rone* ***R****esponse* ***C****ontingency, have isolated them, and soon, they will be captured and returned to the camps where they*

belong. The safety and security of our nation is of the utmost priority to my office; and I assure you that the values upon which we have built this society, that which you have entrusted to me, is well cared for. Thank you."

Satisfied that she had delivered the necessary blow to Tanner's hope for sparking insurgency, and for that matter, entering any doubts into the minds of the people she commanded, V tapped her wrist band and brought up a holographic Visio.

"What is the status of the fugitive, Telanthia?"

"There are no traces of her whereabouts, nor of the other two women who are assumed to be accompanying her," responded the computer.

V turned to look out over the National Mall, quietly sneering at the very idea that Tanner McNeal and his rag-tag band of followers could ever hope to challenge her authority. She felt absolutely no empathy for them. If they died, so be it, the world would be better off. In fact, had it been her choice, she would have let all men fade away.

With a final glance at the abandoned structure in the distance, the great and once imposing White House, she smiled as a word echoed in her head – *Woman EX.*

31

Tanner pushed on, recklessly fast, banging himself repeatedly, but the pain of such was more acceptable than the growing specter of the one-eyed drones catching up to him.

The blast had created a wall of rubble which blocked the passage, but he did not stick around to see how effective it was.

As he squeezed through a narrow chasm in the rocky tomb around him, he suddenly found himself facing the others, who sat or leaned or had fallen to the ground in sheer exhaustion. Beyond them, perched on an elevated rock-ledge, was Mav and the rest of his crew.

A large smile formed on his lips as he approached. “I’m happy to see this sorry bunch .”

“Sounded like you gave them a welcoming party?” said Mav with a mischievous grin.

“Let us hope it buys us time. So, what’s the deal here?”

“This,” began Mav with a wave of his hand, “is the end of the line, Cap.”

“Shit!” said Tanner in a hushed voice. “Any ideas?”

“We have been discussing that very subject. Dep, and his immutable brilliance, has deduced that there must be an underground river nearby.”

"How can you tell?" asked Tanner of the Indian.

Dep pointed a flashlight to the upper part of the cavern. "See that moisture and the moss collecting on that far wall, it is the result of condensation. The rocks are quite wet in comparison to down here, and that tells me that we must be near an underground spring or river of some sort."

Tanner tipped his head at him. "You're suggesting that we might be able to escape by following a subterranean river?"

Dep nodded.

Of course, with the chips being down, and nowhere else to go, Dep's proposition, wild as it seemed, was the only ticket they had.

Matis, being the smallest and most agile of them, jumped to his feet. "Let me take a looksie," he said as he grabbed the flashlight from Dep and then scaled the far wall with the ease of a mountain goat, hopped onto an extruding ledge and then disappeared into a chink – a depression, which to everyone else appeared as just another shadow in the already dark cave.

Moments later, Matis reappeared, shivering, and dripping wet. On his face resided an erasable smile. "Yup, there's an underground river down there," he pointed, "cold enough to shrink your balls too."

Tanner turned to Mav. “Okay, Matis and I will go first. If you do not hear from us, hopefully that is a good sign.”

“Wow, that’s reassuring,” said Mav. “You just make damn sure you get through,” he said with a firm look and a punch to Tanner’s arm.

After descending five or ten meters, along a slippery moss-covered ledge which funneled downward, Matis led Tanner to the edge of an underground river. The water passed by with relative silence, but it was a deceptive silence. As he slipped into its shockingly frigid embrace, Tanner was gripped by a powerful current.

Matis slipped in beside him with a trembling grin. “I didn’t exaggerate, did I?”

They waded through the deepening stream, gaining momentum as they did, until they reached a gap in the wall ahead, where the torrent whooshed off into the steeped darkness with a distant roar that echoed back at them. Tanner waved the flashlight into the abyss, but all he could see were two massive slabs of stone between which the water surged and disappeared.

“What do you think?”

“I think,” answered Matis with trembling lips, “we need to do something before my balls break off.”

32

It felt as if time had not only stopped, but somehow reversed itself, as if they were sitting in a time warp.

"How long do you really have?" asked Tel of Linda.

She had treated enough patients during her medical career to see the signs of imminent death. The sunken skin, protrusive bones, loss of natural color and lackluster, the diming aura in the eyes, all of it flagged that Linda's condition was far worse than she had earlier let on.

"Maybe a month, I don't know," she sighed. "Fact is," her voice sounded frail and distant as she spoke, "I was planning to sit it out until the Grim Reaper came knocking at my door. Instead of that asshole showing up, you came along." She gripped Tel's hand, not wanting to let go.

"Don't you have family or friends who can be with you?"

Linda shook her head. "They are all dead, Tel. Besides, I do not want to die with someone dripping tears over me. When I go, it will be on my terms, with a delightful book in my lap and a cup of coffee nearby."

Tel's eyes teared up as she reached out and touched her frail form. "I'm sorry you had to endure all of this."

Linda shrugged. “I have made peace with it. Besides, look at us. You travelled a bazillion miles to a fucking wasteland, and I survived a nuclear assault and two rocks half the size of Manhattan, and now, we still get a chance to change the world – just like we used to talk about doing. Is that fate or what?”

“I guess so.”

Linda smiled, weakly. “It is time for you and your friends to go. Remember, just follow my instructions.” She nodded at a backpack on the nearby table. “In there is everything you need for your trip.”

When they stepped from the house, twilight had consumed the land.

Tel looked back at Linda one last time.

Her frail form now blended with the lamenting and dilapidated house which was fading in step with her irrevocable demise.

It would be the last time she would ever see her friend.

33

Tanner’s head broke the surface of the brutally freezing water, gasping as his lungs burned and screamed for air.

Submerged in the vortex, for what seemed an eternity, with his lungs on the verge of exploding, was a frightening experience, as the torrent squeezed them between two massive rock shelves – banging them about like ping pong balls.

Tanner was not sure he would ever see the light of day again.

Shaking the water from his face, he realized that he was looking up at the sky. A brazen azure, with a few fleecy clouds surfing the winds high above – and the sight was the happiest sight he had seen in a long time.

Matis surfaced next to him, emitting a similar expletive as he gulped in air.

34

The bus ride from Sag Harbor to Allentown, PA, took six hours, with innumerable stops between.

Every time it braked and jerked to a stop, letting passengers on or off, was cause for a panic-attack for the three women, wondering if at any moment the WG would storm the vehicle and take them.

Tel sat, her head idly bobbing and swaying to the rhythm of the vehicle, watching as the dark countryside rolled by. The monotony of the trip lulled and tempted her to sleep, but her innate discipline and training fought back, refusing to let herself succumb to the call of her body.

Her tired mind drifted along forgotten byways, as old memories, like vintage scrolls tucked away in ancient vaults, their edges wilted and marked with the patina of antiquity, drifted into view.

Visions of happy times with her family, old flings, the milestones of her career, the trials, and tribulations of their journey to Jupiter – all of it a sheer cornucopia of life's theater speeding by her mind's eye. It was as if the very matrix of her soul and her subconscious mind were now collaborating to refuel her hopes and dreams, preparing her for the challenges facing them.

A lifetime ago, when she had applied for the Jupiter Mission, friends and family seemed reserved, their words cautiously reminding her that such a trip, one never embarked upon by any person, could easily end in disaster. Anticipatory excitement overruled their concerns, but once she was in training at NASA, and the reality of their fate went from abstract to concrete, it was then she realized that death was just a mistake away.

Now, she was embarking on another mission, one that held its own threats.

For the first time in years, she recalled the words of the NASA head-psychologist, who had briefed them one day on a subject she called, *Embracing Death,* a bizarre and yet necessary talk about fear and emotion which might grip them in the event of life-threating circumstances, and how they should respond.

"Don't fear death, embrace it," said the women, her words now ringing clear in Tel's mind as if she were sitting in that very room seventeen years ago. *"Space will challenge you. It will challenge everything about you. It will seek to find every misplaced nut and bolt, every weakness, every link that is not firm. Not everything will go as planned. The unexpected will occur, and you will face life and death circumstances, and you must come to terms with the fact that you will be vulnerable. Your best weapon is you. When challenged by dire circumstance, remain clear-headed. Look death in the eye, not as something to be feared, but something to be beat. The dire moments, those that will defy your very existence, will be your most important, and how you perform in those moments separates those who survive and those who become death's victim."*

She closed her eyes, breathing and embracing those very words.

In her light trance, the face of Tanner emerged from the storm.

Somewhere, out there, he was fighting for his life. The man she secretly loved, whom she had secretly loved since they first met.

When her eyes opened, a sign, dimly lit by the headlights of the bus, passed by, announcing that

Allentown, Pennsylvania was just twenty kilometers away.

She poked Rose in the ribs.

"Wake up. We are there."

35

Three lonely figures sat huddled in one corner of the Dunkin Donuts shop, across the street from the bus depot in Allentown, where Linda had instructed them to wait until contacted.

A tendril of light formed a crimson line on the horizon, a welcoming sight to most who were all-too-happy to feel the sun's warming rays; but to Tel, Rose, and Camilla, it was quite the opposite, because darkness and shadows had become their new protectorate – shielding them from prying eyes, security cameras and the dreaded drones.

Their work at Tetra-Drone had provided them with a special insight into the world of Ai and robotics; they understood the true nature of V's army better than most. The drones were equipped with small pellets designed to injure or kill, and they were immensely effective, using state of the art perceptics which permitted them to pick-up sounds, heat-signatures and even identify faces up to a kilometer away. And because they were silent running, the drones could be watching them from anywhere without being noticed.

For those who worked at TDC, robotics was a marvel of the new Utopia. Ai not only dominated and replaced the menial tasks formerly required of people, whether in industry, logistical matters, care-giving and other household duties, they had also entirely replaced the need for a human policing force.

For them, however, drones were a nightmarish reminder of the Orwellian society they found themselves in.

Rose finished off her second donut, washed it down with a swig of coffee and then leaned back in her chair with her eyes fixed on Tel who was clearly caught in the grasp of a mental vortex.

"Earth calling Tel, hello!" said Rose.

Tel turned to her with a small grin – beckoned by a distant call.

"You are way too quiet girl, and way too serious."

"Sorry. I am just worried that if one thing goes wrong with this plan, people will get hurt."

"We don't have time for doubts, Tel," retorted Rose. "Besides, we're enemies of the State now – we either beat them at their game or we end up chipping rocks for the rest of our lives."

Tel nodded. "I know. I am still processing it all. I never saw this in my future."

"Nobody could have predicted this outcome." She waved a hand. "I wasn't expecting paradise when we came back, but honestly, not in my wildest dreams did I expect this crap, and moreover, a woman in charge of this pile of manure."

Camilla chimed in at this point. "I think history will mark this as a turning point."

Rose rolled her eyes with a slight shake of her head. "Please, Camilla, not another history lesson – not now!"

The Argentinian grinned. "No, seriously. Even though it all seems so incredulous and circumstantial to us, that we have become players in a serious game, it is not without precedence. Singular events in history, such as this, have shifted the course of the world – sometimes even overnight."

"Oh, you mean like dropping nuclear bombs on people?" said Rose with a sardonic grin.

"I was more referring to passive movements, like civil rights movements, sudden shifts in the cultural zeitgeist which changed the human paradigm." She paused. "The Resistance believe in their cause, so I think we have to believe in them and hope for the best, not the worst."

36

All but two of the men, out of over a hundred, had unsuccessfully endured the torturous underwater journey. The bodies of the two washed up on the shore, showing they had sustained heavy blows to the head and drowned. They were promptly buried.

In the darkness of night, the string of figures slowly trudged along the riverbank. Despite their hunger and exhaustion, their new-found freedom gave them a sense of hope – like a rope pulling them up from the depths of abysmal apathy where they had lived for years.

For Tanner and his men, it was an exercise in vigilance, constantly on the alert for the glow of neon blue – the dreaded sign of drones lighting up the forest around them.

On two occasions they had sighted them in the distance as they fanned the hills in search of them; and while they were not defenseless against the machines, gunfire in the still of the night would only draw more.

Mav tapped Tanner on the shoulder. “Lights up ahead, Cap.” He pointed.

Squinting into the darkness, Tanner saw the twinkling through the tree line.

“I think that is Ford City,” said Matis, holding the old, tattered map up to the moonlight.

“What d’ya think?” asked Mav.

Tanner looked back at the weary string of men now flopped to the ground. Cal Williams, their elected leader, stepped up to Tanner. “So, we doin’ this or not?”

Tanner nodded.

While everyone remained hunched down in the dark, maintaining relative silence, Mav and Brenner did a quick reconnaissance and returned an hour later.

"You were right, Shorty," said Mav to Matis, "that is Ford City, and the encampment is on this side of those lights," he pointed.

"What about guards and drones?" asked Tanner.

"We saw only two guards, maybe a couple drones watching the place – not much more," answered Brenner.

A plan was born. Using pure guerrilla-warfare tactics, one team would distract and engage the guards and the drones; making a window of opportunity for a second team to enter the camp, free the imprisoned men, grab up whatever supplies of food, nanobot injections and weapons they could find, and disappear.

Success was based on the premise that such camps were lightly guarded, like the one they had been incarcerated at for eight months. Tanner was sure that Lady V, in all her arrogance, would not waste people or money guarding camps from an external assault, one that she was sure would never come.

Considering that men, now weakened by the virus, posed less threat to her regime, the merit of their strategy proved itself.

An hour later, two drones had been shot down, two guards were subdued, and over two-hundred incarcerated souls were now free. The assault had also netted them food, nanobot injections and more weapons.

With their numbers rapidly swelled, Tanner formed three separate groups to maximize their impact and to make it more difficult for them to be tracked.

Over the next week they managed to infiltrate five more camps spread around the lower hills of the Allegheny Mountains – freeing up a total of nine-hundred men – bringing their army up to a thousand in size.

In all, while their ranks rapidly grew, so did their taste for freedom and so did their reputation – one that was spreading by word of mouth, certainly not through the propaganda portals of Lady V's controlled media.

-IV-

1

It had been days since the last sighting of the escapees, and in that time, Lady V often paced her penthouse office like a caged tiger, while poring over reports from the CAB – her intelligence network.

Her mind was gripped by the fact that Tanner McNeal continued to evade her grasp while successfully compromising her camps and freeing more men.

This had never happened on her watch; the fact that men were running amuck, and it was starting to create noise and chatter in the ranks. The word was getting out that Tanner McNeal, a man she had publicly humiliated during the Tribunal, was creating havoc in her domain – and it was sending Lady V's anger brimming to the heavens.

She had underestimated him, and the sense of humility, of being bested by a man, was chipping away at her ego-driven image of immortalized perfection.

Compounding the issue was Telanthia and the other two women, also, somehow, managing to slip through the net.

Ever since the *Cataclysm,* the road she had walked for the last eighteen years had been one of sheer empowerment, with little resistance along the way. She was the hero, the woman behind WIP, the iconic leader championing the new paradigm.

There had been other renegade factions, of course, those who did not see eye-to-eye with her vision for New America, and the Resistance, notwithstanding, but they had been easily quelled by the overwhelming support of her loyal followers and of course, her army of drones.

From the ashes of her old self, the Phoenix had been born. Edna Bright, the eighteen-year-old girl, a victim of sexual abuse and damaged goods, had transformed to the person she was today – Lady V - for Victory; a name given to her, an avatar that spread through the streets, through the city and beyond into other states, as the hope for a new utopia grew – a woman's world.

Now, a worrisome cloud was dimming her victory, because out there was a man stirring up trouble.

2

The streets of Allentown had magically transformed, in just minutes, from night to the light of dawn, and from sleep to abundant life.

People began to appear in numbers, cars formed queues at the streetlight directly in front of the donut shop where they sat – and the world became animated.

Two military-grade Hummers suddenly screeched to a halt at the bus-depot across from them. On the side of the vehicles was the logo of WIP.

The three watched as nervous panic suddenly escalated inside each of them, as WGs exited the vehicle and dashed into the bus depot in clear view from where they sat.

"How did they know?" whispered Rose.

Tel was shaking her head as her eyes followed every movement of the WG and her mind feverishly sought out an answer, because now, they were within clear sight of anyone across the street. If they tried to leave the shop, there was little doubt the guards would spot them.

Their attention was so transfixed that they failed to notice the young woman, the same who had served them, standing next to them.

"More coffee, ladies?" she asked, causing them to nearly jump from their skins. She held up a decanter for them to see, but as she did, her next words shocked them even more. "You need to follow me, now, before they find you."

Without another thought, they surged to their feet and followed the employee to a small back-office, one with its own exit. She handed Tel a sheet of paper and flung open the back door and pointed. "Keep moving that way. Follow those instructions and you will come to an abandoned gas station. Wait there."

Just then came the sounds of the WG crashing into the donut shop.

"Run!"

3

The mandate was written in stone; people were to be at her disposal, day, or night.

In fact, the decree was so inviolate that on the few occasions when it had been disregarded, whether by negligence or malice – all hell broke loose.

As she emerged from her office, taking the elevator down one floor, she was met by a disquieting silence, a corridor that was oddly empty.

Lady V cocked her head as a dissonance reverberated inside, a portentous and disturbing omen.

Stepping to the office of her personal secretary, she flung open the door in an imperious manner and was met by consummate silence.

Marching to the next, and larger office, where a small army of assistants were usually busily at work, she found herself faced by a disquieting tomb.

Where is everyone, she thought.

She yelled, demanding an answer, expecting someone to come dashing at the very sound of her voice, but no one responded – just a death-like silence that engulfed her.

Strutting back to her office, her high-heeled boots clicked stridently against the marble floor - the only sound to be heard, besides that of her hastened and anxious breathing.

"Computer?!" commanded V as she entered her office.

Silence ensued.

"Computer, what the hell is going on?"

Again, there was only morbid emptiness.

Lady V stormed to the window and looked out at the National Mall, the one anchor she always used as affirmation of her power and status as President of the nation.

Her eyes nearly popped from their sockets, gasping at what she saw. The Washington Monument stood there, in its entirety, brightly lit and spiking upwards into the sky as a symbol of freedom; and beyond that, the White House was shining once again, like a beacon in the night.

Her world spun out of control, as if the very ground below her was sinking into an abyss, and she felt a clutching choking sensation around her throat. She gasped and clawed for her next breath, as if a shark had suddenly snatched her into its jaws – clenching and squeezing the very life from her.

The nightmarish scene morphed, as the image emerged from the darkness; the cruel face with those lustful eyes perusing her body, his hands groping at her as the stench of his foul breath filled her nostrils. She clawed at him as he ripped at her under garments, screaming as she did, but no sound emitted from her lips – just the sense of desperate consternation, one that filled her like water pouring down her throat.

Lady V surged up from her bed, her heart pounding so hard that she was sure it would break through her chest.

A thick film of sweat layered her entire body, her pillow and sheet soaked by it, while an uncontrollable trembling riveted her.

She sat there a long time, just breathing, trying to control the shock waves still coursing through her.

When the visions of her nightmare abated, she cautiously slipped from her bed, walking with a weary and watchful vigil, as if that monster, the one who had haunted her since she was nine years of age, might still be lurking in the dark shadows of her room.

Finally, in the relative safety of her bathroom, she looked at herself in the mirror.

Her skin was pale and wet, almost feverish looking.

Her eyes were dull, not the usual self-confident glint that affirmed her unchallengeable power.

Instead, she saw something else - something she had not seen in them for an exceedingly long time.

Fear!

4

Success had fueled confidence in them, but pragmatism now dictated another course of action.

Their sheer size hardly made it difficult to spot them, especially by drones with infra-red scanners, and more difficult to keep fed and armed with weapons.

A decision was made to break the men up into even smaller units of twenty, each of them armed.

Following the same pattern, they were to keep up the assaults into Ohio, West Virginia, and New York State – freeing more men, collecting more weapons and vaccine, and putting a serious dent in V's operation.

Tanner sat with Petar, listening to the silence of the forest around them – an ambience which he found both calming and conducive to their circumstances, because the slightest noise was like an alarm clock going off in this vast domain. Even the sudden absence of normal sounds, such as owls or birds, or the like, was a warning which their ears were now tuned to.

Quietly, they waited for the result of their latest recon. Rizo, one of the men they had recently freed from the camps, was overdue. He had been sent to scout ahead, to check out the next encampment which they could see through the trees from where they sat.

Tanner was quietly reticent. Something was worrying him –a dissonant voice that played on his nerves.

"You think we should ease up tonight," asked Petar, seeing the brooding in his face.

Tanner's eyes peered into the darkness at the flickering lights of the distant compound. "I am not sure what it is, Petar. It is just a feeling."

"Are you worried that passions are running too high?" he asked.

"A little," answered Tanner, recalling to mind that just two days ago they had lost several men to drones during their latest raid. Although they had freed up nearly two-hundred more slaves from that camp, there were losses too.

"I wonder what's keeping Rizo so long?" asked Petar with a nervous glance at the distant compound, and just then, as if on cue, a lone figure appeared, his silhouette barely defined by the backdrop of a quarter moon.

Rizo slipped into the small enclosure. Sweat gleamed on his forehead as he huffed to the ground, catching his breath.

"So, what's the report?" probed Petar.

"It is lightly guarded, like the others, with only three guards walking the entire compound, and two drones. There is a smaller gate off to one side. I saw men carrying containers out and dumping it in a big pile."

Tanner sensed a certain cautiousness about him – the slightest nuance in his body language.

"You seem hesitant," inquired Tanner.

Rizo shook his head. "I'm fine," he answered with a reassuring grin.

"How many men do you estimate are in there?" asked Tanner.

"Judging by the number of barracks, I'd say at least two or three hundred."

Tanner weighed the factors in his mind. On one hand, it was a dark night, with just a quarter moon, perfect for such an assault. On the flip side, emotions were still running high from their recent losses, and that could make men both careless and vindictive. He simply did not want to add to the body count.

"You got doubts 'bout doing this hit, tonight?" the voice of Cal Williams resonated from nearby. He had been listening in.

Tanner turned to him and shrugged. "Yeah, I do, Cal."

Cal pointed a finger at the group of men resting nearby. "You have given them something to live for, Tanner. A chance to fight back against a life of forced labor." His eyes flashed with a passion that shone in the light of the dim moon. "Whatever happens out here, it's all plus to them, and if they die fighting, they died as free men – not slaves." He paused to look Tanner in the eyes. "You're not doing them any favor by denying them another chance to fight for their rights."

Emboldened by Cal's words, Tanner set aside his concerns, and within the hour, two teams were in place.

Peering through his night binoculars, he tried to make out any details inside the compound.

A chain-link fence encircled the entire facility, standing at least three meters in height, with razor-wire layered in two lethal piers, making it impossible for anyone to scale it without being ripped to shreds.

Lights lit up the domain like a Christmas tree, and a thin blue string of luminescence ran parallel to the entire perimeter, demarcating the sensor system used to alert to any movement nearby.

The voice of dissonance echoed yet again.

Something was bothering him, something was wrong, but a distractive cry erupted from within the camp, pulling his attention away.

It was the sign they had been waiting for, as the trash dump located on one side of the camp suddenly flashed and flames reared up, like a beast clawing at the night sky.

5

The three women ran until they could no longer do so, their breaths coming in deep gasps.

They leaned against a wall, looking back toward the donut shop, watching as WGs skirted the building in search of them.

They had avoided being taken by just seconds.

"Let's go!" said Tel, taking a quick glance at the hand-drawn map she had been handed.

Haunted by the vision of the WG, they ran in spurts, walked, hid, and then repeated the same pattern until the abandoned gas station, with its dilapidated and pock-marked sign, came into view, like a forgotten relic from a past age.

Nature was already reclaiming its domain as shown by thick growths of weeds cracking through the asphalt; and the acrid smell of grease and mildew, scents that came with both age and abandonment, saturated the air inside the small office where they hoped to escape the chill outside.

Few cars passed by, in fact, less than five in a period of an hour. They counted every one of them with growing anxiety, but then, the sixth, an aged white van, pulled off the road and stopped by the gas pumps.

As the door creaked open, an elderly woman gingerly placed a foot to the ground and emerged.

She stood there for a moment, her eyes scanning the nearby streets, clearly assessing the terrain, and then, as if she knew they were watching, she turned to them with a smile formed on her lips as she motioned them out.

Once inside the van, she promptly drove off without a word, and after a time, she stopped on a small residential street, distanced from any houses.

The silver-haired, yet well-preserved woman, turned and looked back at the haunted eyes of the three.

"Relax ladies, you're safe."

She had a calm demeanor, and eyes which were both friendly and yet firm.

Dressed in an old trench coat, rubber boots and a hat pulled down over her head, she looked more like a character from a comedy film than someone who would be part of a resistance movement.

"Are you taking us to see the head of the Resistance?" asked Tel.

The woman smiled. "You must be Tel?" she raised a brow.

"I am."

"Well, nice to meet you. My name is Nancy Monroe – some call me Z – and I am the head of the Resistance."

6

Tanner remained hunched down behind a line of trees, watching as the pile of refuse transformed from a small mountain of stinking garbage into a towering and raging inferno – its flames spiking up into the dark sky like dragon tongues lashing out at the stars.

They watched as two guards charged through the side gate, along with two drones, their single eyes scanning the terrain with their blue light fanning and illuminating the ground below as their mechanical brains interpreted the input.

A group of men followed, carrying buckets of water, which they dumped on the fire, evoking a cloud of steam and white smoke.

Gunshots suddenly filled the air as the other team launched their assault.

Tanner was about to make his move when Cal gripped his shoulder and pressed him down. He nodded in silence as the small object, which Tanner had not seen, moved stealthily toward them, like a shark picking up the scent of fresh blood, its indigo light fanned the ground ahead.

When it was just above them, both Tanner and Cal unleashed a hail of bullets at the drone. It weaved and ducked, while unleashing its own assault.

Suddenly it burst apart and smashed to the ground.

Tanner turned to assess the damage and saw one of the men, dead – with a pellet impaled through his eye.

"Fuck!"

Cal Williams did not wait a second to mourn the man – he had seen enough death in his years in the camps to make him numb to its touch. He dashed to the front gate and then snapped it open using a crowbar.

Tanner, Peter and two others charged into the compound, heading straight for a row of barracks.

Stepping up to the first building, Tanner pushed the door open with the tip of his assault rifle, wary that a guard, or even a drone, might be waiting inside – but the building was empty.

It was then that he felt the cold dread sinking into his bones; the same sense of discordance he had felt just minutes before, now touched him yet again, as if to say, "*Told you!*"

He turned, and as he did, drones pressed in on them like wild dogs.

Cal raised his weapon to fire at them but was instantly met by a pellet that impaled his hand. He grimaced in pain as he reached to stem the blood from the wound.

The Visio flashed in the air, displaying the face of Lady V, her lips pressed tightly together in a smug smile and her eyes watching Tanner, clearly reveling in the victory of the moment.

"Stupid, stupid man," she said, "did you really think you would escape me?"

-V-

1

After what seemed an inordinate length of time, sitting in the back of the van, it came to a stop with a tapering moan.

The elderly woman led them into an old farmhouse nestled amidst a grove of pines and set back from the road. Around them seemed to be nothing but vast tracts of farmland.

"Take a load off your feet, ladies," she casually announced as she directed them to a cozy nook, with vintage sofas and a sea of pillows. "I got homemade soup and freshly baked bread. You look like you could use some grub."

Once again, it felt as if they were living in another dimension.

In the space of two days, they had escaped from New York City, travelled to Sag Harbor, cloistered themselves, first in Linda's home, and now, two states away, with the WG on their trail, they were holed up on a farm with the leader of the Resistance – surreal was in fact a charitable term to describe it all.

The house was dark inside, but far from gloomy. Soft light effused from table lamps, while the embers of a fire glowed in a hearth nearby, and a salting of candles here and there that flickered like small fairies dancing in the air.

It was an old, but quaint and charming abode – with generations of family pictures lining the walls, pastoral paintings of country scenes hanging here and there, and a massive bookshelf – brimming with the works of countless souls.

Nancy stepped back into the room with a tray of steaming bread and hot soup, the aroma of which sparked a visceral hunger deep inside them. “Help yourselves. Got more in the kitchen.”

They had not realized just how hungry they were until now. The constant anxiety, fear, and apprehension of being caught had not only drained them, but it had also subdued their appetites. But now, tucked away in this relative Hobbit Hole, they felt safe enough to succumb to the call of their stomachs.

The elderly lady returned with a large pot of coffee and another tray of fresh cakes. It was a mouth-watering festival, and each of them ate as if they had not eaten in weeks.

She added logs to the fire, then sat down on a chair across from them, with a smile and a glint in her eyes.

By all appearances, she could have been anyone’s mother, with her snow-white hair, wrinkled visage, and friendly smile – but there was something about her, an aura of determinate resolve, like you just knew that beneath that veneer of amiability, was a fighter.

"You girls have caused quite a shitstorm."

"Ya figure?" responded Rose while negotiating a mouthful of cake.

"My sources tell me that V is having a very bad day since you three hiked your way out of the Big Apple."

Rose grinned. "I hope she fook'n dies."

Nancy tipped her head. "Now, now, let's remain civil."

Rose raised a challenging chin, flagging that her confrontational side had just had the gauntlet dropped at its feet. "What do you mean, civil? That bitch is Hitler with tits and a vagina – she needs to be taken out."

Nancy raised her hand to the air. "Naturally, she does, but how we go about doing that is quite another matter altogether, and one that defines us as different from her ilk." She then turned to face Tel. "Your boyfriend, Tanner McNeal…"

"My boyfriend?!" exclaimed Tel with a slightly surprised look.

Nancy smiled. "I meant that figuratively."

"It's okay, Nanc… I mean, Z," interceded Rose. "Tel has a big button on the fact that everyone knows she's in love with Tanner – something she doesn't like to admit."

"Ah," said Nancy, "well, your secret is good with me, honey. As I was saying, Tanner has stirred up a serious nest of hornets. He and his men have successfully executed assaults on mining camps throughout Pennsylvania and neighboring states. He has an army of, by best estimates, about a thousand men now."

Rose grinned. "Sounds like our boy."

Nancy nodded. "However, we did just receive some sobering news."

Tel leaned forward. "What?"

"Tanner and some of his men were captured last night when they tried to break into another compound."

Tel felt the spark of hope suddenly quenched.

"Where are you getting all this intel?" asked Camilla.

"As Linda told you, we have been building up the Resistance for years.

"So, you have someone on the inside?"

"More than one," grinned Z.

2

Lady V sat back in her leather armchair with a flippant and victorious demeanor imprinted on her face, not to mention the narcissistic smile which was indelibly molded to her lips.

Two WGs stood nearby with their fingers poised by their gun-triggers.

Tanner was still wearing the same work clothes he had on when they had escaped the mining camp weeks before. He was dirty, sweat-ridden, and a red blotch stained his right shoulder where a bullet had cut into his flesh during one of their assaults.

"You made quite a splash out there, Tanner."

"That was the general idea."

Wearing black leathers this time, she crossed her legs and waited a second or two before continuing, a showy assertion of her control over him.

"Put yourself in my position now, what would you do with you and your men?"

"Let us go."

She chuckled. "So, you can go out and cause more trouble?" She shook her head.

"So, we're the demons in the mix, is that it?"

She shrugged, a cavalier and dismissive motion. "You always have been." She stood and walked. "Must I remind you about our last talk many months ago?" She momentarily glared at him before continuing her diatribe. "Since women took over, there have been no wars, no murders to amount to anything, crime is zero, mass gun shootings, rapes, every single negative statistic that society had to deal with before the *Cataclysm*, is gone. We do not need policing forces today. We do not need standing armies. And we certainly do not need nuclear weapons or others means of mass-destruction. What does that tell you, Tanner?"

"We've already been down this road," he answered.

She tapped her forefinger to her head.

"I'm just trying to get you to wake up and smell the coffee, as he saying goes."

"I could use one right about now?"

Once again, the sequacious grin appeared, as she pointed a finger to the air with a Shakespearian pose. "Remove men from the equation and suddenly, the world is a calm and peaceful place where everyone can prosper." She stopped in front of him. "Isn't it obvious, Tanner, that the very reason men resisted giving us equal rights and equal power in the first place, and treated us like some obsequious little bitches they could leverage their perverse sense of entitlement over, is because they knew in their hearts that we could do a better job than they could?"

Tanner remained silent.

"I think that the power-elite knew to the bone that if they let women take control at prominent levels of governance, corporate and banking and other fields, that eventually our very essence would start to change the nature of the game from a male-dominated one, to something much better." She turned on him, her eyes now firm and hard. "We play to win too, just like you do, but the difference with women is that we don't have to kill and maim and destroy in the process. That is the distinction in our matrix."

"I get it, but…"

"But what?"

"You're a fucking hypocrite, V."

"Really!" she laughed. "How do you figure?"

Tanner's eyes floated up to meet hers. "You say you don't have a policing force or standing armies, and yet you do have the drones – drones that kill."

"Ah," she cuts him off with a flash of her hand, "… you see the drones as a stereotype – I get it." She grinned. "You fail to see the beauty in them. Drones are used instead of people because they are cheap and sustainable, and they do not bleed, or die or require protection. But most importantly, drones have raised the bar on security and justice."

Tanner chuckled. "Seriously – you're playing that card?"

She moved toward him, like an advocate in a court room, ready to launch her dissertation to the jury.

"Drones cannot be fooled. If a crime is committed, even in the event of an accident, a drone records precisely and exactly what it sees and hears. It provides irrefutable evidence in any case. Facts, not opinions. Truth becomes apparent. That is security and justice. They remove the human-error factor, in fact, they remove the opportunity for corruption or perversion of the system."

"Not in the wrong hands they don't."

A laconic grin crept to her lips. “I think that Karma possesses a certain sense of irony, don’t you?” she says as she walks to the nearby window.

“Karma or crazy?!” responded Tanner.

“You can take that moral high ground, but think back, and take an honest look at the world you left when you and your crew rocketed off to the stars.”

She stepped closer, hunching down in front of him – her eyes level with his. “Do you have any idea how it felt to the rest of us, as a mere handful of very ignorant and narcissistic men launched nuclear weapons at each other? Can you conceive of the singular sense of extinction we faced? That sense of visceral oblivion?!”

“Admittedly, no.”

Lady V returned to her chair, sat, and fixed her gaze on him. “That is right, you cannot. But you did cause this to happen, Tanner. Men, collectively speaking, are the reason that in the wake of two apocalyptic events, things went as they did.” She pointed to a map on a nearby wall. “Go to most any nation today, and you will find that leaders and the population in general, all agree on one thing – men cannot be trusted with power.”

“I have heard this speech before. So, you have no intention of ever letting us be anything but slaves and sex toys, is that it?”

Her brows furrowed as she tipped her head to one side. “I find it insultingly humorous that you’re accusing me of that, when, before the *Cataclysm*, that's exactly how we felt in your world, Tanner."

Her eyes drifted momentarily.

She continued. "God, if there is such a being, must have a perverse sense of humor. There we were, on the edge of self-annihilation, the ultimate technological highpoint of humanity…" her voice echoed hauntingly in the room, "… and yet, completely unable to stem the destructive impulses deep inside the few who were about to sacrifice the whole human race just to satiate their perverse egos. God, the Universal All, the all-powerful, the omnipresent, the Divine voice …" she threw a hand in a sweeping arc. "…pitches a couple of Earth-shattering rocks at us and changes the whole damn playing field." Her grin widens. "What do you think, Tanner, is that fate, Karma, the work of Divinity – or was it just bad fucking luck for you guys?"

Tanner stood as anger flashed across his face, a move that caused both guards to sweep in.

"Let him speak," she said with a wave of her hand. They stepped aside.

"You're telling yourself a nice story, V, and you've told yourself that story so many times that you believe it's the truth."

"What story is that?" she asked.

"You think you are saving the world. You are just putting it on the road to another disaster. The thing is," he calmed himself as he searched for the right words, "I empathize with you and every woman out there who had to endure the shit that the patriarchy put you through. In fact," he smiled, "when NASA and the ESA were picking the crew for the mission to Mars, they planned only one woman on the team, and I insisted on no less than three."

"Are you trying to warm up to me, Tanner, make me think that you're a fan."

"I would not think of it. I am just telling you a fact, that most men are not what you think. True, the world was out of balance, and we can blame the handful of assholes who fucked it up, but in truth, we were all to blame, even you. The crime of omission, our complacency in letting leaders take power, people who did not belong anywhere near such offices, in permitting those nuclear arsenals to accrue at a maddening rate, that's on all of us. You can pretend it was just men, but in that, you would be and are deluding yourself."

She watched him with a humorous glint in her eye. "Nice speech, very moving." She circled the room before continuing. "By the way, we both know the prime reason for your mission to Jupiter was a stepping-stone to something else - right?" she tipped her head at him. "NASA was smart enough to see the writing on the wall – I will give that to them. They could not stop the nukes and the global warmongers, or insane governments from going fist-to-fist, or even global warming, but they could find us a new home, a fresh start, and your mission was the springboard to colonizing an exoplanet – right?"

He remained silent.

She wagged a finger at him. "Unfortunately, it was a failed mission from the start. A false hope. You know why?" She lingered. "Because a predominance of power in the hands of men is and always has been a cocktail for disaster. Even if your mission had succeeded, even if an exoplanet were found, one we could colonize, how long would it take for men to fuck it all up again." She shook her head. "As far as I'm concerned, those rocks did us a great favor."

She paused. "And by the way, I know about *Footprint*."

Tanner felt a slight shockwave streak through him.

She grinned. "Oh, do not act so surprised, Captain. I had a team crack your ship's computer. Did you really think you were going to hide that from us?"

"What are you going to do with that information?"

She shrugged. "Not sure, but it's certainly not a priority right now."

"Ah, so just keep everyone in the dark about one of the greatest discoveries ever, that we're not alone in the Universe."

She flicked a hand at him. "What do you think I should do with *Footprint*?"

"Make it public knowledge, of course. NASA is, or at least, was a public agency…"

"NASA doesn't exist today."

"Nonetheless, knowledge of *Footprint* could change everything, how we see our world, religion, you name it."

Her brows flicked upward. "Which is exactly why it will remain a secret for now."

"Don't rock the proverbial boat – uh?"

Her mood shifted, becoming more somber. "Even though you don't deserve it, none of you, I am going to give you time to consider one final offer."

"Which is?"

"Go on camera and admit to the nation that what you did by breaking out and causing all that havoc, was wrong."

"Why would I do that?"

"Because, I would be willing to mitigate the sentences of all those men you broke out of the camps. I have studied your file, Tanner. I know you care about others, more than you care about yourself. Otherwise," she tipped her head at him with malice in her eyes, "my drones will hunt them down and show them no mercy. And, if you refuse…" she tapped her wristband, causing a Visio to appear, "…these three ladies will not be shown any mercy either."

Tanner's jaw tensed like a vice.

3

Nancy Monroe sipped on her coffee while eyeing Tel with an inquisitive look.

"Humor me please," she began with an amiable smile. "How is it possible that you three appear so young, considering your years in space?"

Tel answered. "We were in sub-sleep-stasis for most of that time. It slows the physiological aging processes. On top of that, zero-gravity puts less strain on the human body."

"Amazing. You don't look a day over thirty," she said with a wave of her hand. "Anyhow, I am digressing. Tell me your concerns about what I have told you so far."

"I don't understand how you intend to overthrow V without using an army of equivalent force?"

Nancy smiled. "Ah, the pragmatic scientist speaks."

"In my defense," continued Tel, "I spent most of my career studying the observable, and idealism wasn't part of that."

"Okay," said Nancy as she placed her coffee cup on a side table. "You are relatively young, all of you, so I'll grant you some margin of doubt," she glanced at the other two who listened on. "History of the human race, at least what can be deciphered from all the fiction, shows us that lasting changes were not based on the amount of blood spilled, but on the dynamics set in motion which brought about a shift in the foundational zeitgeist of a culture – how the collective mind thought. Take a well-known one, the civil rights movement, led by Dr. King decades ago, to overturn discrimination right here in America. He had numbers on his side, but not force. King appealed to a much stronger dynamic, one that resided within every human being, white, brown, or black - the desire to be free and to be seen as equals. In the same way that he leveraged that power to turn the civil rights movement into an unassailable force for change, V manipulates it for her own agenda."

"How?" asked Camilla.

"When nuclear bombs wiped out millions, and then two rocks hit us shortly thereafter, it was post-apocalyptic on a level that is hard to conceive, a traumatizing event that impacted every human being; and frankly, it was people like V, and others around the world, who jumped up on the soapbox and started mobilizing recovery efforts. You must realize, the infrastructure of our society, as we knew it to be then, was in disarray. Governments had collapsed, men were dying faster than flies, and no one was in charge – and I do mean that."

"You mean V wasn't always a sick bitch?" said Rose with a raised brow.

"No, in the early days she was iconic – a figure that others rallied around."

"You were with her?" chimed Tel with a look of sincere surprise on her face.

"Yes. In those days, we all worked together to fix things. The nukes, the rocks and then…"

"The virus?" said Camilla.

Nancy nodded. "You have no idea how shocking it was to suddenly find men dying, first by the dozens, then the hundreds, then it was off the charts. Panic set in. The end-of-the-world idiots were out in the streets with placards chanting their doomsday mantras. It was, to be blunt, a fucking nightmare. In the middle of all that, **WIP**, got into motion here in America. Women began to realize that if they were going to survive, they had to band together, so under the banner of ***Women in Power***, V became the torch bearer for a new hope. I was already actively mobilizing women in Delaware, where I lived at the time, so naturally, I hooked up with her group, and that was the beginning of what is now the largest party in the nation."

"WIP couldn't have been the only group going?" said Camilla.

"No, it was not. There were other movements across the nation, and of course, elsewhere in the world, but WIP caught on fastest in America and dominated. It was not a fanatical organization in those days. V's mantra was simple, we had to take over from men, because in the months that followed, it was clear that the virus, unless stopped, was going to push the gender over the edge. Women had to jump in and take over all manner of infrastructural functions. It was a game of tag, *you're it* where we had to learn what we did not know, and fill holes left vacant by the guy who was there the day before."

She sighed as memories moved in, like a slow rolling fog, threatening to pull her back to a distant time. She shook her head.

"Unfortunately, V lost her way, and I'm pretty sure it was volitional on her part."

"Why do you say that?" asked Tel.

"I know her background, I know what happened to her as a child and teen." She paused. "I watched the radicalism take hold, as she became known as Lady V or Victory. That is when she started dreaming up this Utopia of hers – that is when this fanatical side came into play."

"But I thought she was developing nanobots to stop the virus?"

Nancy's head rocked. "Oh no, my dear, she wants people to believe that, but in truth, it was other leaders, from other nations, who put together a team of geneticists to find that serum that saved what was left of the male gender – and believe me, it was not a minute too soon, because by that time, we'd lost the majority of men to the virus." Her eyes dimmed slightly as she sighed. "Lady V made a showy gesture of being involved for political reasons alone, but secretly, I know she hated them and wanted to let them all die."

"Now I hate her even more," said Rose, a flash of anger exuding from her eyes.

"It is easy to hate people, Rose, and much harder to retain one's compassion for them. V is not a monster by her choosing. She did not choose the life she had led, even though she could have made other choices – better ones. V is the product of a composite trauma, one that is so powerful that it drives and compels her to do what she is doing, an internal force that makes her believe to her very core that what she is doing is the best possible solution for all." She raised a brow at Rose. "You called her Hitler – and the analogy is not entirely incorrect, because even Hitler, the most hated human being in recorded history, was also the byproduct of the social system around him, those who helped mold the monster we came to know.

Nancy paused.

"V was sexually abused by her own father, who repeatedly raped and pillaged her body. She lingered a moment. "He was the real monster, a heinous man who violated a young girl from the age of nine until the day she turned sixteen."

Nancy's eyes drifted up to meet theirs. "On her sixteenth birthday, Edna Bright, which is her real name, waited for him to sneak into her room one night, baiting him to do his usual with her, and when he was off-guard, she drove a knife into his eyeball and deep into his brain. It killed him instantly."

"Fook me!" exclaimed Rose.

"And she got away with it?" posed Camilla.

"Indeed, she did. Her mother, who had ignored the desperate pleas of her young daughter who tried to tell her repeatedly, that her husband was a sexual predator, was forced to spin a story for the police or let her daughter go to prison. The point is that she was the victim of dehumanizing sexual abuse– and those scars are deep, very deep, so deep that they drove a sixteen-year-old girl to commit murder."

"How did you learn about this?" asked Tel.

Nancy smiled. "Oh, she told me her story one night, early in the movement. Looking back at that time, it was a slip in her defenses, or maybe she just wanted to tell someone, and since I was a loyal member of WIP at the time, she confided in me." She paused, looking them hard in the eyes. "Make no mistake about it, Edna Bright died on that night as she happily watched her father in the throes of death. She has evolved since then, and the woman that we know today, Lady V, hates men with a passion you cannot begin to fathom. She wants the power because she is obsessed with never letting it fall into the hands of men, and this compulsion has driven her to do the unthinkable."

Their silence was an invitation for her to continue.

Nancy's head rocked back and forth, her eyes reflecting a wave of incredulity breaching her shores.

"One of our members, a plant inside V's camp, recently discovered something which has compelled us to step-up our plans to make a move against V. It is called Woman EX, a research project that V commenced with a team of scientists about five years ago. The goal is to create the perfect woman, in fact, the androgynous woman."

"Wait, what?!" exclaimed Rose. "You mean a woman that has both sexes?"

"No, not in the sense of having both male and female genitalia, like hermaphrodites. I am referring to a woman who is genetically modified so that she is capable of independently spawning children, both male and female, without intercourse, without artificial insemination – in other words, without the need of men ever again."

"How far is she along with this research?" asked Tel.

"They've already gestated Beta prototypes and they are not far off from closing the circle."

Silence reigned as they all tried to reconcile the implications. Camilla broke it.

"So, once she has Woman EX coming off the assembly line, she's created a whole new breed of human."

"Yes," responded Nancy. "But there's more…" she paused, tipping her cup to her lips, and taking a sip.

"Our informant also discovered that while reconfiguring the female genome to create Woman EX, her team found a cure for the virus killing off men."

Now the shocked looks were as flagrant as bright lights on their faces.

"You're saying she has the answer to the virus and she's withholding it from the world?" said Rose, her voice escalating in crescendo.

"If our information is correct, her team have not only found a way of stopping the virus, but in fact, in reversing the effects of it."

"Which means that men could be cured."

Nancy nodded.

"Now you understand who we are up against and why matters have escalated as they have. V hates men to such an extent that she will never permit that cure to become public knowledge; and once the sperm banks around the world run dry, no further procreation will be possible – the human race will be on the clock, inevitable extinction in the not-too-distant future. V will introduce Woman EX as the answer, and I guarantee you, despite any shock, the world will accept it as the only solution to ensuring the future of our race. That is the legacy she wants to leave behind and that is why we have to act now to stop her."

4 Two weeks later …

"So…" began Rose, "her voice carrying a tinge of doubt as she stared at the dark highway ahead. "You really think our girl can pull this off?"

Tel shrugged, trying to keep her focus on driving the van and not on all the things that could wrong with the plan that Z had laid out for them.

Rose continued with her usual immutable and confrontational approach. "We're putting the entire future of the Resistance in the hands of one computer nerd."

"She's one of the best."

"Was!" emphasized Rose with a flick of her brow. "How do we know that her skill set will work today? It has been twenty-years since she hacked computer systems."

"True, but she's a smart cookie, she'll pull it off."

"I would feel better if…"

Tel cut her off. "You know, sometimes you can be a real pill."

Rose smiled. "Ah, finally, a sign of aggression from the Buddha herself."

"You really enjoy confrontation, don't you?"

Rose shrugged. "Better than social platitudes and the ass-kissing that most people engage in."

"I prefer taking the higher road."

Rose chuckled. "You think because I challenge shit that I'm taking the low road?"

"No, but I do think you enjoy going fist-to-fist with people."

"And you prefer avoidance."

Tel sighed. "I don't feel uncomfortable with conflict."

Rose paused, reflective for a moment. "Where I grew up, you either showed you had spine and could stand up for yourself, or you got the shite kicked out of you." She paused. "Anyhow, that doesn't change the fact that everything in this plan is dependent on our Argentinian comrade," she nodded at Camilla who was fast asleep in the back of the van.

Tel drew in a deep breath. It was not as if she did not have her own doubts, but at the same time, she knew that they had to do something fast, because Tanner was now back in the hands of V, and besides, the whole Woman EX scenario continuously played on her mind like an imminent zombie attack.

5

A thick fold of murky autumn clouds smothered the land, its cold tendrils reaching down to the very thicket of trees where Mav, Matis, Brenner and twenty other men were cloistered.

A small fire burned, not enough to warm anyone, but adequate to heat water so that each man could imbibe a cup of instant coffee – the meager remains of their plunders.

Food was running short. It had been weeks since they last attempted an assault and for good reason too, Tanner had been captured and they were reticent to press Lady V's patience.

Brenner poked a stick into the fire, shifting the embers and splashing sparks into the night air, and then piled on more dry branches.

"We'll find them, man," he said, his eyes reflecting his undying resolve.

Mav looked up at him. "I know," he said, forcing himself to put on a face that he was not accustomed to wearing. Now, more than ever, he appreciated the burden that Tanner had carried for so many years. It was easy to lead others when everything was on the up-and-up, but when men were hungry, when every decision could make the difference between life and death, and when he had to be the anchor and inspiring force in the face of impossible circumstances – it was different.

As the hours stretched on, and as the cold continued its endless assault, the others fell into a fitful sleep. Mav took the first watch.

The ambience of solitude and desolation of the wilderness around him brought back memories of Europa, a place where he had experienced silence that was so profound that the noise in his head pounded, like drums, in comparison.

A faint rustle caught his attention.

Mav shot to his feet, gripping the cold hilt of his gun.

Again, it came, this time to his left. He spun in response and stepped toward the sound with his gun aimed into the darkness.

"You better announce yourself before I start shooting," he threatened.

A lone figure emerged from the trees. "It's me, Rizo."

6

Tel looked up at the behemoth, Tetra-Drone Corp, the forty-eight-story slate-black structure that speared upwards into the Manhattan skyline on Water Street.

A shudder shook her, not from the cold, but from the very idea of entering that building again.

She parked the van in Battery Park, just walking distance to TDC.

It was early morning, and the city was still in the clutch of a thick fog.

Tel scanned the area one more time. Everything seemed normal. The Staten Island Ferry had just rumbled to a stop nearby, churning up waves which knocked against the dock announcing its arrival. Overhead, a jet roared on its final approach to JFK International Airport, while a string of early morning cyclists rolled by.

As always, the Big Apple was alive, day or night. The only thing missing in this otherwise, "normality," was men. She had not seen one since arriving in Manhattan.

She turned to face Rose. The Welsher could not betray her consternation. Her face was drawn and taut, like stretched leather, and her eyes flicked nervously as she stared ahead.

"Are you okay?" asked Tel.

Rose drew in a deep breath. "Yeah, I'm just fook'n peachy."

Tel grinned. "We will be waiting for you by the back exit, as planned. Good luck!"

Rose quietly slipped from the van and checked her coat pockets for the contents they had picked up along the way.

Moments later, she successfully evaded a score of New York cabbies who sped along Water Street as she negotiated her way.

Nervously, she walked the entire length of one side of Tetra-Drone, her eyes darted up and down the mostly vacant street, wary of every movement and sound, and mostly that of drones.

With an edgy glance over her shoulder, she ducked down the back alley and slipped behind a row of dumpsters; waiting and calming her frantic breathing, all the while anticipating that a hidden camera might have compromised her and that guards were heading her way at that very moment. But there was nothing - just the subtle harmony and backdrop of a city slowly awakening from its slumber.

Peeking around the corner of the bin and seeing nothing, and no one, she lifted the lid to the nearest trash container, squirted a copious amount of lighter fluid from a small can she had in her coat pocket, then she repeated the same with the other two bins.

With a final look, up and down the alley, she lit up each bin and then ran.

7

Rizo sat hunched over, with his arms wrapped around his knees. His thin frame appeared more like a crooked branch in the light of the fire which flickered nearby.

A patch of caked blood adorned his forehead, arousing deep concern from Mav, Michael, and Matis who sat huddled nearby, waiting for him to speak.

"So, what the fuck happened?" asked Mav of Rizo – his patience finally giving out.

Rizo drew in a deep breath and released it slowly. He looked up at them with a face that revealed something dark, something painful. "It's my fault," the words squeezed past his lips as ripples of agony and guilt washed over him.

"What are you talking about?" asked Michael.

"I'm the reason Tanner and the others were captured."

They looked at him, their brows furrowed and their eyes suddenly ablaze with a mix of confused emotion.

"I took a deal from V."

Brenner lurched forward, a crazed look of rage in his eyes, and smashed into Rizo, crushing the man to the ground, and then punched him repeatedly before the others managed to drag him off.

Rizo remained down, clearly a broken man, a guilt-ridden one, with the laceration in the side of his head now spilling out a renewed gush of red and his lip cracked from the blows he had just endured.

Mav stood over him – his own fists balled up in repressed rage. "You better start talking before I let Brenner finish what he started," his voice growled.

Rizo gingerly pushed himself from the ground, smearing blood on the back of his hand as he wiped his face.

"Tanner sent me to do a recon on a camp. While I was sneaking around, a guard stepped out in front of me." He paused, his eyes dropping to the ground as shame poured in. "Next thing I knew I was sitting in a room talking to Lady V on a Visio."

"What did that bitch offer you?" asked Mav.

"She said she wouldn't have me shot on the spot if I helped them ambush Tanner."

"So, you took the cowards way," exclaimed Brenner as he stepped forward - his large fist balled up like cannonball.

Mav raised a hand. "Hold on, Michael" he said as he hunched down in front of Rizo. "How'd you escape?"

Rizo expelled an apathetic sigh. "As soon as they caught Tanner, two guards marched me out to the woods," he said with a sneer. "That bitch had no intention of honoring the deal." He lingered a moment.

"I was sitting on the ground waiting for them to put a bullet in my head when I heard a thump. When I opened my eyes, the guards were unconscious and one of your guys was standing there?"

"Who?" asked Mav.

"The Indian guy."

"Dep?"

Rizo nodded. "Yeah, I think that's his name."

"Dep saved your slimy ass?" said Michael.

"Yes…" he answered with his head still slumped. "But then, when I told him what had happened, he pointed his gun at me and told me to leave and never come back."

"And yet, you found your way to us, why?" asked Mav.

Rizo looked up at him with sorry eyes. "I can't live with what I did – I need to make good on this."

8

Three trash bins roared with flames as the angry tips of the inferno flashed upwards, scorching the backside of TDC, and setting off alarms.

Employees rushed down the stairwell, a fire exit from Tetra-Drone Corp, frantically pounding out of the building in response to the fire alarm that blared.

Tel, Rose, and Camilla remained out of sight – waiting for their chance. When the exodus had waned, and with everyone still gripped by the panic, they easily slipped through the door, dashing up the stairs, a long and tiring hike to the twenty-fifth floor, the very hub of Tetra-Drone's mind.

Fortunately, someone had wedged the door open, allowing people to rush out of the massive control room.

They entered without issue, and for the first time in their tenure at TDC, they found themselves inside the matrix, the very heart and soul of V's robotic world, a place that only those with the highest security rating could enter.

The room, easily half the size of a football field, was awash with a literal sea of computer stations, while massive LCD screens adorned every wall.

As they stood there, momentarily mesmerized by the sheer titanic scope of the facility, a small shape silently emerged at the far corner of the complex – its blue scanner systematically fanning the area.

Terror suddenly gripped them.

9

The forest was dark with thick undergrowth, and every step reminded them that they were cold and hungry.

It was not as if they had a choice in the matter. They couldn't use the roads, the drones and WG would be watching those, so they had to stay on the fringes, the confines of dark forested areas, crossing streams and rivers, trudging through wet grass, all the while accosted by the boney touch of a cold autumn wind that seemed to blow ceaselessly, as if surviving wasn't already hard enough.

They had managed to find food in an abandoned warehouse, tins of tuna which satiated their hunger, but that had been well over a day ago, and now their stomachs ached for something more.

"Where the hell are, we?" asked Mav, pausing to catch his breath.

Matis squinted at the remains of the old map in his hand. Age notwithstanding, the map was soggy and ragged from constant exposure to rain and dew. He looked up to the night sky, his eyes following the patterns of the stars.

His years of training as an astronaut, moreover, the years spent in space, had given him the mental acuity to visualize roads in the sky, as clear as the ones on the map in his hand. Arcturus Constellation pointed westward. Delphinus was east, Scorpius pointed south, and finally, Polaris was north.

With a raise of his brow, he answered. "My best guess is that we're here," he pointed to the map, "somewhere around Cherry Tree or North Cumbria."

"Which means we've covered about thirty clicks in two days. It's going to take weeks to get to DC at this rate," said Michael with a tired voice.

Mav knew he was pushing the men hard. Too hard at this point judging by the looks on their faces and the stoop of their bodies. Two of the men they had recently freed from camps, had died just the day before, expiring from a terrible flu that had suddenly gripped them. Without the means of injecting them with nanobots to fight the virus, there was little else they could do but watch them fade away. And more would die, that was inevitability. From Mav's perspective, they had to fight and fight fast, and if there were no more vaccines to be found, it would be their last fight.

"We should find food and camp down somewhere. It will be dawn soon," said Mav, his eyes scanning the thick mantle around them.

“There’s something over there,” answered up one man, pointing to the sparkle of lights that dimly flickered through the trees like fireflies.

Sure enough, it was a house, set apart on its own.

Following a short reconnaissance of the property they easily accessed the house and found themselves inside a warm and inviting home.

Judging by the ample supply of fresh food in the refrigerator and canned goods on the shelves, and the scent of recent wood-burn coming from an open fireplace – its owner could not be far away.

The temptation to leave, for safety’s sake, was compelling, but as Mav looked around at the men, their haggard and drawn faces, pale from exhaustion, hunger, and constant exposure to the cold, and the constant battle against the virus that waged war on everyone’s bodies, it presented its own counter argument.

An hour later, with their stomachs full, the men fell into a deep sleep.

Brenner and Matis returned from having searched the entire house for weapons or phones. “Nothing,” announced Brenner.

Mav sighed, but no sooner had the breath wheezed from his lungs did they see the headlights of an approaching vehicle illuminating the darkness outside.

"Shit!" said Michael with alarm in his voice, "…we gotta go!" he said as he turned to wake the others.

"No, wait!" responded Mav as he pulled back the curtain and peered out. An inner sense was telling him that to bolt now would be more disadvantageous than simply dealing with it.

He watched as the vehicle came to a stop and a woman stepped out clutching two bags of groceries. As she walked toward the house, she stopped dead in her tracks.

"Shit, she knows," said Mav as he dashed for the door and flung it open and stared into the face of a very pretty redhead.

"We're not going to hurt you," he announced with his hands held in the air, as if to show his intent.

"We just needed some food and a place to stay for the night and then we'll be gone."

She lowered the bags to the ground and smiled at him.

"I figured you might show up here – that's why I stocked up."

10

Gripped by an overwhelming and nauseating sense of terror– as if death itself was about to pluck them from the world of the living – the three women stood stone-cold.

The drone moved with a deathly silence, casting its ever-constant fan of light ahead of it, and then suddenly it too stopped – its ocular dome spinning to face them.

In that moment, mere nanoseconds of time, the three prepared themselves for the worst.

The drone charged at them.

When it was upon them, an explosive concussion filled the room, and the droid, just a meter or two away, shattered into countless pieces, spilling its guts like bags of marbles crashing to the floor.

Still shocked at their near miss, they stood there, momentarily stunned, as a figure emerged from behind a bank of computers. She wore the typical suit of the Women's Guard; black leathers, black riot helmet, black everything; not to mention a formidable weapon which she easily hefted in one hand.

She pulled the helmet from her head and smiled.

"You don't really think Z would send you in here without some backup, do you?" she said matter-of-factly as she reloaded her weapon.

"So, you are part of the Resistance?" asked Rose.

The woman shrugged and holstered the gun. "Of course, otherwise you'd be dead by now." She pointed to the large console to the right. "That console accesses the mind for the entire drone network. Do your magic and be fast about it; as soon as the fire alarm ends, this place will be filled with people again."

She put her helmet back on and disappeared into the stairwell.

Camilla fished for a paper from her pocket, one that Z had given her before leaving, which she had pored over during their trip to NYC. The print-out provided coding, obtained at a dire price, which for someone with the right skills, such as Camilla, could be used to hack into the guts of TDC's mainframe computers – at least, they hoped that was the case.

She started tapping the keys, her fingers moving with a speed and dexterity that was impossible to follow. Her eyes worked rapidly back and forth between the paper and the screen.

Suddenly the blare of the fire alarm disappeared.

"Better hurry, Cam," said Tel, listening with one ear to the stairwell as voices started to echo upwards.

After another agonizing moment, she exclaimed. "Got it! I am through the first level security system," she declared. "Give me the key."

Tel rummaged in the backpack and pulled out a small device that looked like an old-fashioned flash drive and handed it over. Camilla plugged it into a port on the console. "I hope this works," she said, her eyes reflecting the depth of her anxiety.

The key, according to Z, was designed to decipher the computer language used by Tetra-Drone, translating it to a binary language that Camilla was familiar with from her time. Without it, the computer language used today was sufficiently foreign to her that hacking into the brains of TDC would be next to impossible.

"Come on, come on!" said Rose, her eyes nervously glancing back at the door as the pitch of voices grew louder.

Suddenly the screen morphed from an obscure digital language, to one that Camilla instantly recognized. "It worked," she announced as her fingers raced over the keyboard. She opened a file that appeared, entered a series of commands, watched, and waited as the machine responded and then typed in more coding.

Camilla felt the old buzz as adrenaline pumped into her system as she raced through the cyber corridors, evading dead-ends, jumping digital hurdles – a maze that to most would have been hopeless to navigate.

It was pure piracy, the lust for plunder, and for her, the victory of breaking into yet another secret vault and showing her proficiency. If the moment had not been so critical, she would have savored it.

"How much longer?" asked Tel with a nervous hitch of her brow.

Camilla did not answer.

The sound of voices suddenly emanated louder from the stairwell.

"Shit, people are coming," announced Rose, her face wrought with fright.

Camilla's eyes were riveted to the small icon which blinked repeatedly as the program processed her commands.

Suddenly, the door opened, and a crowd poured in – silence ensued as their stunned gazes fell on the three intruders.

"Step away from that station," a voice commanded loud and threatening, as a WG plowed through the crowd with her weapon drawn and aimed at them.

A wave of sickening panic gripped Tel as the computer announced, *please enter your password.*

As the WG walked directly at Camilla, she remembered the words of the NASA psychologist during their preflight training – *"Don't fear death, embrace it and then beat it."*

"Finish it, Cam," screamed Tel, and then she tackled the approaching Guard, crashing into the woman and knocking her to the ground. As they struggled and thrashed on the floor, another guard rushed forward, her taser aimed directly at Camilla who was now punching in the final password.

Seeing what was about to happen, Rose pitched herself into the path of the taser, taking the full brunt of the dart which sent her crashing to the floor as an excruciating jolt of electricity spasmed through her.

As the altercation ensued, Camilla pressed ENTER and turned just in time to receive a blow to the head.

11

Although each tried his best not to reveal their emotions at that moment, their anticipation gently played across their faces like leaves rustling in the wind.

Their host, who had first shocked them with her cavalier statement, and then introduced herself as Serena, had marched by them, insisting as she did, that before any further discussions, fresh coffee and dessert would be served. Hospitality was still alive in this part of the world.

It was a picture that floated somewhere between surrealism and fiction for them; as if at any moment, talking pigs would appear, or Elvis himself would show up, or an alien would join them for a cup of coffee.

They had been living in a world that bordered on Orwellian up until now, and the very fact that this woman had not instantly and at once jumped in her car and dashed away to report them to the nearest authorities, was itself a novelty that each of them was still trying to reconcile.

Was it a trick, wondered Mav?

Was she playing them?

Or maybe she had already reported their presence and was just biding her time until the WG showed up?

As he watched her studying the body language of the redhead, he sensed that her intentions were authentic – not disingenuous.

The other men in their beleaguered crew remained fast asleep in the other room, evidenced by the orchestra of snores emitting; entirely oblivious to what was happening.

With a tray of fresh donuts and the aroma of hot coffee taunting them, Serena nodded and waited with a pleasant smile on her lips, as they feasted.

Moments later, with the subtle echo of satisfied stomachs, she spoke.

"I guess you're as surprised to hear that I am not your enemy, as I am to see you sorry-looking lot in my house," she began, her tone conveying a humorous nuance.

"We haven't exactly been welcomed since arriving back to Earth, you're pretty much the first," said Mav.

She tipped her head with a flick of a brow. "I know – it must be a shock."

"This is Michael and Matis," began Mav, "… and… well, you know who I am. How is that, anyhow?"

She flicked a brow. "First of all, we do not see men around these parts anymore – and certainly not a group this size. Besides…" she paused, "… Tanner McNeal and his crew of intrepid space jockeys are practically celebrities – biggest news to hit the airwaves in a long time," she grinned. "I recognized your face from the Tribunal and the tabloids."

"Ah!" nodded Mav. "That fucking kangaroo court."

"Indeed. Lady V's idea of justice."

"You didn't seem surprised to see us, why?" asked Matis.

"We knew you were somewhere in the area. There are more people tracking your nighttime raids than just Lady V and her goons."

"Like whom?" asked Mav.

"The Resistance of course," she announced with a pretty smile as she took a sip on her coffee.

"The Resistance?" chimed Matis.'

"Yes," she smiled. "I'm part of an underground counter movement."

"What does it do?" asked Mav.

"Up until now we've just been recruiting, building up our ranks and placing people in strategic positions to help forward the cause."

"What cause?"

Her pretty smile accentuated her rosy cheeks. Brenner was captivated with her and seemed to be making no secret of the fact as he sat entranced by her every gesticulation.

"Like you, we want to bring back the balance."

Mav leaned back, crossing his arms as he did.

"Balance?"

"Restore equality between men and women."

"How exactly do you define balance?" challenged Michael.

"Equality, in every aspect of society. No more male-dominated power-hierarchies, no more gender distinction or objectification – a true balance, which is our goal."

"And how do you plan to make that happen?" pressed Brenner.

"Actually, the wheels are already in motion as we speak."

12

Serena continued.

"We could not launch the full Resistance before now because we did not know how to deal with the drones. There can be no revolution if those things remain under V's control. So, we have been working on ways of infiltrating Tetra-Drone."

"Tetra-Drone?" said Matis with a confused look.

She shook her head. "You guys are really in the dark, aren't you?"

Mav shrugged. "In our defense, we've been shoveling shit in a mining camp since coming back to Earth."

"TDC or Tetra-Drone-Corp is the matrix of the drone network. TDC is headquartered in Manhattan."

She paused, momentarily reflective. "Anyhow, we tried to compromise their system more than once, and we paid a heavy price each time. Now, we have a new weapon."

"Which is?" asked Mav.

Serena flashed a smile. "Someone you know, someone from your crew actually."

Confusion swept over his face. "Who?!"

"Camilla. She is quite the computer genius."

Mav leaned forward. "Are you telling me that Camilla is part of the Resistance now?"

"Actually, all three of your former female crew mates are involved. While you were chipping rocks, they were integrated as part of the robotics development program at TDC."

They looked back and forth at one another, truly shocked by that news.

"So, what, they just took off?" asked Michael.

"I don't have the full story, but from what I understand, they were pretty sure that the President was going to use them as bait to lure Tanner into the open, so they made themselves disappear."

"And ended up with the Resistance?" said Mav.

She shrugged. "Fate has a strange sense of irony, I know," she said as she sipped on her coffee.

"Anyhow, all that aside, they've been on the lam, and magically, through an old friend of theirs, who also happened to be one of our loyalists, they ended up at the door of the Resistance leader."

Mav smiled, shaking his head in disbelief. "But why them?"

"I'm told that Camilla is exemplary in the field of computers."

Matis waved a finger in the air. "Oh no, she is more than that. She was a legendary hacker back in Argentina. In fact, she hacked into NASA computers just for fun, almost lost her ticket onto the *Dauntless* because of it."

"Well, she is our great white hope right now. If she can infiltrate their main frame and disable the computer system, we will have time to launch the revolution without the threat of drones being used against us. If not, people will die, and the revolution will be crushed."

"I thought V was all about being the great protectorate of women?" mused Brenner.

A sneer formed on her face. "She is not that principled. She has a line – and she will cross it if it means protecting her power; we have lost good people who stepped over that line in the past."

"You're putting a lot of stock in someone you don't even know," said Mav.

"I guess we are," she paused, "… but that decision was not mine to make."

"So, how exactly does this all play out?" asked Mav.

"First, we disable the drones, then we take down the power grid so that V can't talk to the nation using her prime broadcasting studio; and meanwhile the Resistance leader gets on the airwaves in Atlanta, Georgia, using a secondary broadcasting studio which we already have people in place to take control of – and if all goes according to plan, the whole nation, in fact, the entire world, will be hearing our message and not V's."

Mav sat with a confused look patched to his face. "You're basing this entire revolution on a peaceful message?"

She nodded. "Yes. We are appealing to something deeper inside each woman. Just like other movements have done in the past."

"Wow, good luck with that," he said.

"You're not convinced," she said with a tip of her head and slight challenge in her eye.

Mav raised a hand. "I'm not an expert on revolutions, but I'm pretty sure it's going to take more than a live broadcast to get those women to get their heads out of the sand."

She grinned, obviously not affected by his skepticism. "I realize this doesn't fit your paradigm for a revolutionary approach, but a lot of thought went into this, and we have agreed amongst ourselves that a peaceful approach will have the most impact in the long run."

"So, what's your role in the Resistance, you seem pretty informed?" asked Michael.

"My job is to take down the Pennsylvania Power Grid, the PPG."

"And how exactly are you going to do that?" asked Brenner with a not-so-subtle flirtatious grin.

"Well, considering that I have been the director of the PPG for the past eight years, and I have placed loyal members of the Resistance in key technical positions to help me, it should not be too hard.

That will take out the power grids in the entire tri-state area – a massive blackout which will keep V's face off the televisions long enough for us to get our message out there."

"Why not just kill the juice at TDC – wouldn't that be easier?" asked Mav.

"TDC has two back-up power systems, a primary and secondary, both capable of powering that building for days, not to mention the fact that the building is tightly monitored and guarded. And those back-up power-systems are located underground, so to destroy them would end up hurting or killing people in that building."

"A small sacrifice to stop V," said Matis.

"We're revolutionaries, not terrorists." Her face assumed a resolute aspect.

Mav was trying to weigh everything up. "What happens if our girls fail?" he asked.

Serena lightly shrugged. "Nothing good, I'm sure."

A moment of silence ensued. Serena leaned forward looking them in the eyes.

"You're going after Tanner, aren't you?"

Mav nodded.

"We have some eyes and ears inside The Center…"

"The Center?" asked Brenner.

She grinned. "Boy, are you out of the loop. *The Center* is the new headquarters for the seat of government in New America. According to our source, Tanner is being kept in a holding cell three levels underground, but you will need to move fast if you want to get to him before she moves him, or worse."

With a cautious peek through the curtains, she continued. "You have still got a good five or six hours of darkness. If you leave now, you can be in DC before dawn. You will want to make your move while it is dark."

Serena stepped to a drawer, took out a set of keys, and tossed them to Mav.

"There is an old delivery van in the back – belonged to my dad. You will find cans of gasoline in the shed as well. And…" she paused as she walked to a small cabinet, opened it, and then released a trip which exposed a cache behind. "My dad collected this for a rainy day - you might find some of his stuff useful."

Mav looked through the opening at shelves stocked with guns and munitions.

13

Lady V charged from the elevator to the heliport, like a bullet shot from a gun.

Her fists were balled up, white-knuckled, as pure hot rage streamed through her like rocket fuel.

A cold October wind whipped at her, flinging, and twisting her long hair into strands resembling snakes on the head of Medusa.

She stepped up into the helicopter, followed by her four most trusted guards, and within seconds, it swept them upward, banking a hard left, and then headed straight for New York City.

An hour later, she arrived at the control room of TDC, madder than a bull in a fight.

Her Women's Guard fanned out forming a lethal wall behind her.

"Who is in charge here?" she commanded.

"I am," answered a woman, her voice cracking as she meekly stepped forward.

V locked on her, like a missile guidance system. "How long before it is fixed?"

The woman hesitated as panic gripped her. "We do not know yet. We are still running anti-viral programs to find the bug."

V's upper lip trembled as the storm of fury raged inside. "You have fifteen minutes to figure this out, or you will find yourself in a mining colony.

The woman nodded with a tremble and turned to a crowd of technicians.

"Take me to them," commanded V of her lead guard.

The door to the small office blew open as Lady V flashed into the room like a flood screaming down a torrid desert canyon. She glared at Telanthia, her teeth bared, like a rabid dog.

"I should have followed my instincts and gotten rid of you when I had the chance."

Tel remained silent as V stepped closer, her arms crossed over her chest with immaculate authority as she probed each of them with her angry eyes.

"Nothing to say for your treachery?"

"Frankly, I'd do it again, bitch" said Rose with a defiant smile.

V nodded at a Guard who promptly marched to where Rose sat and jammed a taser into her neck. She toppled to the floor in a fit of anguished convulsions as Tel and Camilla watched on in horror.

Without a thought for Rose, who flailed about on the floor, V circled the room like a tiger silently sizing up its prey, finally coming to a stop at the head of the conference table.

“I know you think that you just dealt us a blow, but I assure you, that system will soon be back online and then I am going to make sure that the Resistance disappears forever.”

“You think you can stop them?” said Tel.

“Of course, I do. I have known about Z and her merry band of losers for years.”

“Then you also know that they are everywhere and that they’ve infiltrated every level of your utopia.”

V’s eyes narrowed. “And like lice they can be ferreted out too.”

Tel leaned forward. “Am I permitted to speak freely or is your puppet going to taser me too?”

V lowered herself into a chair. “I’m not making any promises.”

“You underestimate the power of the women you are up against.”

V huffed with a patronizing chortle. “Really. So, you are an expert on the Resistance now? And how is the old bitch, Z?”

“I guess you’re about to find out.”

V waved a dismissive hand to the air. “Every time they’ve shown their faces, I’ve clipped their wings.”

“You didn’t do a very good job of it,” retorted Tel, feeling the same confrontational spirit she had accused Rose of demonstrating. Even so, her words skimmed by the President’s ears as the woman’s attention was suddenly drawn to the team on the other side of the glass wall. It was clear now that she was unhinged by having lost control of her drones.

“I don’t get this hatred you have for men,” said Tel, stealing a glance at Rose who was now easing herself back in her chair. Her face was pale and sickly-looking, and she still trembled from the attack.

“I could care less about men,” answered V without taking her eyes off the flurry of motion beyond. “The world is better off without their ego-centric bullshit,” she answered.

“You mean, by creating Woman EX?”

V turned to face her and smiled – a self-satisfied gesticulation. “Ah, so you’ve heard about my little project?”

“Hardly a plan for perpetuity.”

“You’re missing the beauty of it.”

“Really? Replacing women with a genetically modified version, while letting men die off, even though you have the means of reversing the effects of the virus – that is low, even for you!”

V accepted the challenge, as if Tel had just dropped the gauntlet at her feet.

"You're just like those stupid women in the Resistance, clinging to a Jurassic mindset," she declared with an imperious flick of her wrist. "Do you really think that the Resistance is going to *bring back balance to the world*?" She huffed. "Do you really think that men will change their ways and concede to equality, to having women as their equals in every respect?" She waved an angry hand to the air. "Restore men to power, and within years, they will leverage their sense of entitlement again."

She sneered as her lips pressed together.

"You're all dreamers and misplaced optimists in a world that can never be."

"So, Woman EX is the new matrix, is that it?"

V tipped her head. "It has certainly got more prospects of long-term survival. If Mother Nature or the Universe suddenly unleashes another assault on us, Woman EX may be our only hope."

Tel shook her head. "If I didn't know the bigger picture, I would almost buy your bullshit."

V's eyes narrowed as she pointed a finger.

"Careful, you're already on thin ice with me," her eyes twitched with a nervous tick as she turned to look at the TDC people beyond, anxiously awaiting a thumbs-up from them.

"You still haven't answered my question, why do you hate men so much," asked Tel, recalling what Z had told them about the abuse endured by her as a child.

Lady V paused before answering. “It is obvious. Men cannot be trusted,” the hate in her voice intoned in every word.

“It is not obvious to me. In fact, I have met women out there who do not express the hate that you seem to have, and in fact, who do not really have a reason to hate men, but who have bought your propaganda about how evil and dangerous they are.”

V’s eyes drifted back to Tel’s, and her lips twitched as her eyes fluttered with a tentative and passing glimpse at something, a theater that only she was looking at inside her mind.

“Why do you try to hide it - why not let it all out?”

Anger rippled across the President’s visage as she answered. “You do not get to ask me that question. In fact, I ask the questions here,” she snarled.

Tel pressed on. She had nothing to lose at this point. “You were sexually abused, weren’t you?”

V’s palm crashed to the table as her eyes widened, and her nostrils flared with rage. “I told you, stop.”

“I’ve seen that look before in the eyes of abused women – it’s the kind of look you don’t forget.”

V jerked an angry hand to a guard standing behind Telanthia. She promptly pressed a taser into her. Tel hit the floor in a convulsion of pain.

"You bitch, try me, just you and me," shouted Rose, rising from her seat as the same guard then sent her flailing to the ground once again.

"Get those two out of here!" she commanded, pointing to Rose and Camilla. "And wait outside, I want to talk alone to this one," she nodded at Tel, who was still gripped by spasms.

As the painful shock waves abated, Tel eased herself onto the chair, while a horrible feeling of nausea accosted her.

She fixed her eyes on the other. "You can taser me all you like, but it won't change what I see," her words quivered.

"You don't know shit," V arrogantly shot back, but despite her bravado, the scent of fear was now manifest in her eyes, as if her deepest secret was about to be revealed.

Breaking off eye-contact with Tel, V stepped over to the nearby window, looking at the New York skyline for a long time before finally speaking again. When she did, her voice was hushed, it was not the authoritarian tone of the President of New America, nor the assertive and brash icon of WIP – it was a closer version of herself.

"Have you ever been raped?" she asked with a faint whisper.

Tel shook her head. “No.”

Lady V’s lips pressed together, evidence that she was trying to push the memories back into a vault deep inside her head – but something inside compelled her to speak anyhow – as if in telling her story it would embolden her and show Telanthia that she was the virtuous person she believed herself to be.

“It started when I was nine. He would sneak into my room late at night. At first it was the slow caresses, then came the groping, and all the while, the hushed warnings that if I mentioned this to anyone, he would hurt me and my mother. By the time I was ten, he was violating me, sticking his dick into places it did not belong, and that abuse went on until I was sixteen.”

Her eyes glossed over as if the memories had suddenly transported her to another time and place altogether.

“My nightmare became my reality. I hated my life. I hated myself, and I hated him more than was possible. I considered suicide more than once, but the idea of letting him win sickened me even more than the thought of death.”

V turned with her arms crossed over her chest.

Why she had lowered her defenses and suddenly revealed her trauma, Tel did not know, but it revealed the truth about the woman, the pain that drove her and just how systemic it was.

V stole a momentary glance through the glass-wall, at the covey of technicians, as their fingers frantically worked keyboards. Then she looked back at Telanthia.

"I tried telling my mother about it, but she refused to accept the fact that her husband was an animal and sexual predator. I could not talk to friends, school counsellors, or even the police, because I was terrified of the consequences. So, I endured the pain, the humility, and the degradation of being fondled and fucked by that pig."

Her face rippled with waves of hatred, waves as clear as those rippling over an ocean, as she lingered on the moment.

She approached and leaned her hands into the back of her chair. "Have you ever killed someone?"

"No."

V continued to speak as if transfixed to the moment.

"It was my sixteenth birthday. The day of my independence," she declared with a sweep of her hand.

"I sat for hours in my room, debating two options – run away from him or deal with it." Her eyes narrowed as she leveled them at Tel. "Want to take a guess at which one I chose?"

"The second one."

"That's right! When the little pig came groveling into my room that night, I waited while he fondled my perky little breasts, while his putrid breath grew hot with lust, and just when he was fumbling with his belt, I grabbed the knife I had under my pillow, and I shoved it into his eyeball – I shoved so hard that it went through his brain and struck the back of his skull." She let out a long breath, as if reliving the moment with renewed triumph. "I watched the pig take his last breath, as his blood spurted out all over me. It was liberating."

V stepped closer at that point – her eyes fixed on the other.

"Do not think for a minute that I am telling you this to evoke your pity. I am not. You wanted to know why I hate men, now you know."

She stood straight with her jaw pressed forward, a show of authority, as she spoke. "I am glad that pig is dead. I am glad I murdered him. I am glad that he raped me for seven years. You know why?" Her eyes burned with passion. "Because it gave me the strength to do what needed to be done, to rid the world of a sickness called men!

"So, you're not about to release the cure for the virus, are you?"

Her smile slithered across her lips. "That should be clear by now …"

A Women's Guard rushed into the room at that point, cutting her off. "Ma'am!"

"What?" asked V with a snap of her head.

"The Resistance is broadcasting to the entire nation."

14

The truck lumbered down Interstate 270, wheezing and huffing like an old man about to expire.

Matis cast a watchful eye in the rearview mirror as he drove, maintaining a constant vigilance for any signs of detection, or worse, drones.

They passed Bethesda, just outside the Capital, and as they did, The Center, the gleaming polished steel and glass tower, shaped like a stiletto, loomed like an obelisk planted on the landscape by an alien race.

It was still early morning, before sunrise, so the streets had not yet transformed to their usual busy and clogged arteries.

As they turned off the 390 onto Interstate 29, the White House, in the distance, appeared as a dim and shoddy shell – a mere shadow of what it had once been. It was the first time they had seen it since leaving the planet eighteen years before, and the moment was an assault to them.

"Where is the Washington Monument?" asked Matis, his eyes worked the landscape as if he had missed it.

"It's gone," announced Mav, resigned to the fact that Lady V was obviously intent on wiping out the vestiges of the old world.

As they continued southward, drawing closer to their exit, large billboards loomed with the emblem of Lady V's party prominently lit up.

In the back of the van, huddled and squeezed in like sardines, sat Brenner with the other men.

On their quiet, yet pensive faces, was written a narrative, the one that each of them was thinking about at that instant. They understood that they were fighting for their freedom. They understood the price it might cost them – a dear and ultimate one. And yet, in their eyes he could see the same defiant resolution that burned in him – freedom was worth any price.

Watching as the streetlights blurred past and as the traffic began to thicken toward the city center, Mav afforded himself a moment of reflective self-doubt.

Taking on the nation's Capital building, with the President herself holed up inside and certainly an army of WGs and drones guarding her, with only a handful of men, seemed pointedly suicidal. And yet, if he had ever considered the magnitude of the mission that he and the others had embarked on so many years ago, the odds which were stacked against their success of surviving Europa, and then returning to Earth, and the unknown elements they had to face and endure all those years, that too could certainly have been dubbed a suicidal undertaking. And yet, they had succeeded.

All his life he had pushed the edges of the box, refusing to abide by the rules of mediocrity, never accepting a *No* or a *Can't be Done* as more than an opportunity to prove that anything was possible if you had the will.

And now, he faced a challenge that had only two outcomes, and the one they wanted had all the chips stacked against them.

15

Nancy Monroe, Z, stood, stoic and proud, in front of the cameras, her voice echoing lightly inside the studio as the broadcast went out nationally.

Arriving to this moment had taken over a decade of dedicated and selfless work – years of secret meetings, the quiet permeation of the message of the Resistance, constantly seeking out others of like mind, living in the constant fear that V and her network of spies were always on the lookout – and the loss of good women along the way, those who had been exposed and had disappeared into some dark realm dictated by V.

Now, as she faced the cameras, looking at a large screen showing the thousands upon thousands of women who had flocked to Atlanta, themselves members of the Resistance, the moment was historically profound.

Watching from the perimeter of the studio stood dozens of women, each of them members of the movement, who worked at this very station and who had been instrumental in helping to make the live broadcast possible.

Outside, thousands crowded along Centennial Olympic Park Drive, in downtown Atlanta, home of the former CNN broadcasting studio, now dubbed the WMB, the Women's Movement Broadcasting.

In homes, offices, and countless locations around New America, in fact, other nations too, the broadcast went viral as people were glued to their mobile phones, handheld devices and televisions, watching what amounted to an insurgency in the making and a declaration of war against the regime.

Z's words echoed around the globe.

"Lady V has attempted to create a Utopic society, one where women dominate, where women rule and where men are relegated as mere pawns. Many of you listening will have grown up in the post-Cataclysmic era. You know only what you have been told about the era before. You have been led to believe that men are evil, that the world was on the brink of

destruction because of them, and that New America, under her charge, is the best of all worlds. And while it is true that power was severely abused by men, it is not true that they are innately evil. They are humans, just like you. It is the culture that shapes and breeds evil in people, just like the culture of today is shaping your minds through ideology and propaganda."

As she spoke, cameras panned over the faces of the silent throng outside the studio.

"We are the Resistance. We are not terrorists. We are not womanists. We do not hate or regard men as lesser than us. Our goal is to change the cultural matrix, to bring a natural balance back to the world, one where people live as equals, where power is not disbalanced or abused, where war, crime and hatred are not part of the fabric of our society - a paradigm that assures our future as a race."

She lingered a moment, before saying her next words – the most shocking and powerful words of all.

"For some time now, Lady V has had a secret project in the works. Unbeknownst to you, a scientific team has been working to alter the genetic blueprint of women, to produce what she calls Woman EX, the perfect androgynous woman. Her ambition is not only to replace men and make them redundant and extinct, but to replace you as well, all of you, with a new breed

of woman, one which is capable of self-reproduction, one that can perpetuate the new breed. Shockingly, we also discovered that during their research to create this perfect woman, this team discovered a cure to the virus which has caused billions of men to perish, and which today holds them captive. Lady V has kept this cure from the world because she does not want men to survive.

She paused and her ears were met with silence.

If there had been a way of catching the audible shock of millions of women now hearing this, it would have exploded like the roar of thunder escaping the heavens and shaking the very Earth.

She continued.

Lady V will tell you that she has the best interests of humanity in mind, but I challenge you to ask yourself this question; if she succeeds in this endeavor, what will remain of our race in the future? What value will women have and what role will they play in a society where neither the true woman, nor the true man are necessary. Is that the Utopia you want? Do you want your children growing up as the inferior race, as the freaks, as the dysfunctional ones, just as men have been relegated?"

The crowd outside the studio, and across the nation, roared.

16

The plot of land, formerly the location of the East Potomac Park, was now home to the towering structure, *The Center*, a building which cast a shadow over the Thomas Jefferson Memorial nearby.

It was the brink of dawn, but the spotlights still lit up the monolith that cut into the early-morning sky like a knife.

"Do we shoot to kill," asked Rizo, his eyes gleaming with anticipation, anxious to make good on his treachery.

For a moment Mav paused, thinking about it. There had been blood spilled during their raids of the camps. Both sides had lost people. Now, more than ever, he sensed that the blood-loss would be greater. They were attacking the heart of the beast itself, and for that matter, he was intent on freeing his friend at whatever cost.

Rizo continued to look at him, waiting for Mav to answer. The man had betrayed them, and yet, Mav felt no animosity toward him. Instead, he saw Rizo as the product of the very system they were fighting. A human being who had been relegated to a life of slavish servitude, who knew no other life until just recently. While Mav could hate him for what he did to Tanner, instead, he felt empathy.

He turned to face all the men now crouched in the shadows around him. "If it is a question of you or them, shoot to kill – because they will not hesitate to kill you. But remember, our job is to get Tanner and the others imprisoned in that building, not to create carnage."

He turned to Matis. "Brenner and I will go in first with five others, you cover our backs, and make sure no drones get by you."

"Gladly," saluted Matis with a playful grin.

Mav squeezed him on the arm, silently wondering if this would be their last meeting. "Be safe, my friend. I expect to see you on the other side of this."

Matis nodded. "You too, brother."

The plan was both bold and reckless, but nonetheless, Mav was relying on the fact that Lady V, in all her usual arrogance, would have no reason to suspect a threat to her needle in the sky. What he did not know was that V had already taken off, and was now in New York City, all because of Tel, Camilla, and Rose.

Mav stepped out from the shadows and approached the main doors of *The Center*, making no attempt at hiding his presence.

He peered through the tinted glass at two night-guards, waving long enough for them to get a good look at his face, and sure enough, they gawked, their eyes growing wide as they instantly recognized him.

They charged, guns raised, and as they did, the rest of his team flanked him, and unleashed a barrage of gunfire into the thick glass-plate windows.

Shards of crystal exploded inward, a literal wall of lethal ice that rained down on the approaching guards, sending them crashing to the floor and covering their heads.

Mav stepped through the shattered entrance. "Keep an eye on those two," he said as he and others sprinted for the stairwell.

They charged down the stairwell, as Serena had told them, and crashed through the door, coming face-to-face with two more guards who were caught by surprise. As the women raised their weapons, Mav and Brenner already had their guns leveled at them. "Your choice," said Brenner with a grim aspect. They disarmed the two with ease.

"Where is he?" demanded Mav as he pressed his gun to the face of one of the guards. Her eyes flitted nervously as she pointed down the corridor.

"First cell."

Mav pushed her ahead of him until they came to a room, and sure enough, there inside, sat Tanner, Petar, Cal Williams and two other men.

17

Lady V watched in silent horror as her nemesis, Z, spoke unhindered to *her* nation through another nationally televised station in Atlanta.

Every word from the Resistance leader was like a knife repeatedly stabbed into her chest.

"Shut her down!" shrieked V to a panel of technicians who frantically tapped away at their keyboards.

"We can't, they've locked us out from that station," responded the lead technician.

V flashed an angry hand in the air, "Then get me on-line so I can televise now."

The same woman responded with eyes filled with sublime terror. "We can't do that either ma'am; access to the Baltimore station is cut off right now because of a power-outage."

V fumed, as her entire world tremored, like a massive dam starting to crack at the edges.

Her Captain of the Guard approached. "Ma'am, I've just received word that *The Center* is under attack."

Her eyes widened with shock. "Attack?! From whom?"

"A group of men."

The screech that emitted from her, a hollow and painful scream, like that of a wounded animal, paralyzed everyone in the massive room.

V suddenly unleashed a torrent of fury, tearing into a nearby computer station, and sending a keyboard crashing into a wall.

Her fiery eyes and flaring nostrils took away all the glamor from her iconic face and replaced it with the look of someone on the threshold of a breakdown.

For a time, V stood there, her body stiff like a rod, and her fists balled up.

Slowly, her eyes drifted back to the screen, watching as Z delivered her speech.

Her hatred went white hot as she turned to her Captain of the Guard.

"Call out the 2nd Battery."

18

The WG pushed the crowd of technicians to one side of the room, setting up four chairs facing large wall-screens.

The President sat in the chair to the far left and then commanded. "Bring those three out here."

She waited until Tel, Camilla and Rose were sitting next to her, facing the same wall of screens.

V grinned with self-delight. "I wanted you traitorous bitches to witness the end of the Resistance, and…" she paused to flick a brow at Tel, "the end of Tanner McNeal and his ragtag team."

Tel felt a shockwave cut through her like a bomb exploding in her very heart.

Lady V continued, beside herself with a displaced ecstasy, as she lightly tapped a pad on her knee, speaking as she did. "You see, a smart tactician always has a back-up plan." She turned to Tel and the others. "I kept a reserve of drones elsewhere, at an old air force base in Virginia, and that contingency is not monitored through Tetra-Drone. They are controlled by me, and only me, through this," she proudly proclaimed as she eyed the pad.

"What are you planning to do?" asked Tel, watching as the silent storm grew in V's eyes. There was no doubt in her mind that the woman had come completely unhinged at the prospect of losing her grip over the nation.

"Watch and see," answered V as she tapped the pad. One screen came to life with live footage streaming from a drone which sped over roof tops. It took only seconds to determine that they were looking at the Capital, as *The Center* was silhouetted against the light of a morning sun.

The drone dipped down, streaking toward the shattered ground windows, and then charged past the men who desperately tried to shoot it down; but it easily navigated past them.

Everyone watched as Tanner, now freed from his prison, looked up at the drone with instant shock. His demeanor suddenly morphed from the momentary ecstasy of his new-found freedom, to now, dread, as the drone projected a Visio with the face of Lady V. Her eyes feasted on them.

"Silly, silly man, Tanner McNeal and his team of clowns," she began.

"We really have to stop meeting like this," he said, resorting to humor for lack of any other approach to their circumstance.

V cackled with a perverse sense of empowerment, as if the very moment was a declaration of her immutable authority.

"Well, I promise you this, it will be our last," she said. "You are not getting away this time, Tanner. As we speak, there is an entire regiment of drones – two hundred of them, outside the building you are in. You cannot hope to escape and trying to do so will just end in bloodshed – your blood." She grinned with vampire-like delight.

To those watching the bizarre dialogue unfold, it was a disturbing revelation, a glimpse into another side of their iconic leader, one they had never seen before.

"What do you want?" he asked.

V raised the pad in her hand, capturing the faces of Tel, Rose, and Camilla, sitting next to her. Tanner's jaws tightened.

"The deal is simple, Tanner. You call off your boys outside, turn yourselves in, and I will mitigate the punishment for all of you. You can live your life out as you were before. Refuse, and these three treasonous bitches…" she nodded with a hateful sneer at Tel and the others, "… will find no mercy, and moreover," she lingered as she tapped the pad and brought up another Visio for all to see, "that crowd of insurgents you're looking at will feel the wrath for their treason."

Like Dr. Jekyll and Mr. Hyde, she spoke with cold dispassion as she casually played with the lives of people on the bargaining table.

Tanner's eyes were fixed on the thousands of women crowded on the streets in Atlanta.

"What am I looking at," he asked.

V pointed a finger into the Visio. "That is the Resistance, a group of seditious women who have just declared war against the nation."

Tanner turned to look her firmly in the eyes. "You're putting this all on me?"

A sardonic grin spread across her lips. "It is on you, Tanner. You planted the seeds of revolt, and like all men before you, you do what men do best, you fight, you kill, and you create disorder." She leaned back in her chair. "I am simply restoring order and balance."

"By threatening the lives of innocent women?"

V waved an angry hand to the air. "They are far from innocent. You don't turn on your own government and expect to be treated with civility."

"So, if we turn ourselves in, you won't harm those women out there?"

V nodded.

"I'll do it on the condition that Tel, Camilla, and Rose, are not punished. They go back to living their lives as normal."

Lady V shook her head vehemently. "Absolutely not! They infiltrated this facility and attempted to sabotage it; they are in league with the very people now declaring war against me. I will mitigate their sentences, nothing more."

Tanner crimped his jaw. He was backed into a corner, and he did not know how to get out of it. In the seconds that followed he weighed up the choices facing him – fight, or save Tel and the others, and prevent a massacre.

"Okay…" he began with a sense of defeat creeping in, when suddenly a scream erupted from the other end and Lady V's face disappeared from the Visio.

Tel surged from her chair, throwing herself into the President and knocked her to the floor with a heavy thud. The pad skidded across the tiles, coming to a stop in front of Camilla who promptly grabbed it and smashed it repeatedly before a WG put a taser to the back of her neck and sent her catapulting into a fit of spasms.

V screeched like an enraged animal as she struggled to free herself from Tel. Guards pried them apart. "You bitch, you will pay for that," said V as she looked at the shattered pad. “Get me another one, now!” she commanded.

In that instant, as the screaming and fighting erupted at the other end, Tel’s message was clear, she wanted him to fight, not to give in to V’s demands and that was good enough for him.

With just a twitch of his brow and a nuanced look in his face, Mav got Tanner’s meaning and swung his gun upward, firing rounds into the drone.

-VI-

1

Nancy Monroe felt terror streaking through her entire body and soul, a horror she had not witnessed or felt since the first air raid warnings had sounded with the impending nuclear attack and then again, in the final moments of dread, the sheer consternation, seconds before the asteroids struck the Earth years before – a time that now seemed so distant.

Now, her eyes were fixed on the swarm collecting above the women who crowded the streets outside the studio.

At first, there was a growing crescendo of alarm, as fear permeated the thousands who stood there, looking up as the ominous cloud of machines descended toward them.

Z's first impulse was to rush outside and tell them all to disperse, to run for cover, but then something happened, something so transcendental, so surrealistic, that it riveted her where she stood.

The alarm suddenly faded.

As if by tacit consent pervading the minds of every woman out there, the fear which had cloaked their faces suddenly dissipated, like smoke in the wind, replaced by a firm resolve, a statement that they were not about to be cowed into submission.

Nancy felt a depth of pride that brought tears to her eyes – but the power of that moment, the sheer magnitude of their aggregate, yet silent voice, was suddenly shattered as the rain of pellets skewered them from above.

2

Tanner and the others bolted, skidding to a stop as a drone suddenly appeared, charging down the stairwell and spraying a deadly swath of pellets at them.

Brenner let off two rounds, scattering the one-eyed droid into a dozen pieces.

"This way!" yelled Tanner as he headed for an open elevator just as two more drones appeared.

They dove into the elevator, Mav, Brenner, and three other men, as Tanner hit the button.

Like sharks moving in for the kill, the drones sped at them, unleashing their assault, a lethal hail that cut a hole through one man's chest. He was dead before he hit the floor.

The elevator surged up the tall structure, and when the doors opened, they found themselves staring into an immense space, Lady V's personal domain.

The entire wall facing outward was one massive stretch of tinted glass that ran the entire length of the building.

To their dread, drones had already amassed outside that very window – like throngs of rats they threw themselves against the glass plate.

"Get behind something, now," screamed Tanner, and just as he did, the drones smashed through the window and poured in, ejecting a torrent of deadly pellets, like claymores exploding at close range.

Tanner and Mav grabbed hold of V's large polished-steel desk, flipped it on its side, and pressed against it to avoid the onslaught.

Drones scudded the air above and around them, their pellets rapidly taking their toll as they cut into the men below.

Pools of red amassed across the floor, as bodies, punctured with countless holes, poured blood out like sprinklers.

They shot back at the machines, sometimes hitting one or two at a time, but even so, the battle was an impossible one to win against so many.

Tanner fired until his clip was empty. He fumbled to reload it, but his blood-soaked hand caused the clip to slip from his grip. He watched as it skidded across the floor.

As the pellets continued to rain down, the cluster moved in for the final kill.

Teetering on the edge of unconsciousness, Tanner caught sight of someone rearing up next to him.

Rizo, bleeding from more holes than could be easily counted, stole a quick glance at Tanner, smiled, and then pulled the clip from a grenade he held in one hand and tossed it into the swarm, just as a hail of pellets ended his life.

The explosion ripped a hole in the air, sending dozens of the machines to their death, while countless pieces of metal and plastic skewered the room, like shrapnel from a bomb.

In the seconds that followed, with their ears still ringing from the concussion, Tanner managed to look up at the cloud of smoke and particulates, and there, descending to within just a meter of himself and those next him, were more drones – relentless in their duty to finish their mission.

3

After discovering that Tanner had been ambushed, which Rizo had freely confessed to, Dep had determined that the best thing he could do was to head east, to Washington DC, sensing that Lady V would want to keep her trophies nearby.

He was not a specialist on human behavior, he was a scientist, but logic dictated that a sociopathic dictator like Lady V would want to take the opportunity to reduce her adversary to nothing.

With just a handful of men escorting him, they entered the city by night.

Once they had crossed the Potomac, he noticed a sign pointing to the *Joint Base Anacostia-Bolling Airforce Base*, and once again, for reasons he never tried to explain, he decided to follow his nose and they turned and followed the signage.

JBAB, formerly a strategic defense-point for the Capital, considering that it is located just south of the White House and a mere thirty second hop to provide air-defense to the nation's governing powers, had, since the *Cataclysm*, sat idle.

Military aircraft had become redundant; there were no wars to fight, no threats to defend the nation against, no terrorism and no men to fight and kill other men in senseless conflicts. And given that the unilateral disarmament of military forces across the globe had reduced standing militaries to a bare necessity, the base was home to only a handful of operative planes, overseen by just a handful of civilian, not military, personnel.

As the light of dawn peeked through the distant line of clouds, they breached the rusted fence that offered a modicum of security for the base and arrived at one of three large hangers.

As they jimmied the doors to the first hangar, Dep's jaw very nearly hit the floor.

There, before him, stood the *Dauntless*.

He caught his breath at the sight, momentarily stunned at seeing something he never thought he would see ever again.

He had no idea how and why the ship was there; he could only assume, since they had no pilots to fly such a craft, that Lady V had ordered the ship transported to DC where it would be under her watchful eye.

The old bird looked good.

Scorch marks blighted her skin, the vestiges of their re-entry to Earth, but otherwise, she appeared intact.

With his small team of men guarding the hangar, Dep entered the ship and activated the computer.

"Computer - analyze bio-feed for all crew."

Given that the ship's computer was already tasked to maintain a constant vigil on the crew-bios, using RFID chips implanted in each of them, it rapidly assessed and reported back.

"Captain, McNeal, as with Maverick, Michael Brenner, 1st Engineer - Matis and 2nd officer - Petar – have sustained life-threatening injuries."

"What is their location?"

The Visio appeared instantly.

"Ready the ship for take-off to that location," he commanded.

Within minutes he was seated at the control panel with the other five men strapped in behind him. "Auto-pilot on."

"Confirmed," responded the computer.

"Navigate the ship to that exact location where Captain Tanner is and remain in hover-mode."

The ship's quantum drives suddenly whirred with a loud hum, followed by a whine that ramped-up to a high-pitched scream as her engines burst to life.

Within seconds, the ship was rolling forward.

Once it cleared the hangar doors it jumped into the sky, its massive tonnage leaving the ground like a feather suddenly lifted by the wind.

Streaking over the city, the White House passed by in a blur and in just seconds, *The Center*, a structure that Deptha had never seen before, let alone known of, loomed.

The ship slowed as it approached.

"Zoom in on that cloud around the building?" he asked the computer.

The Visio zoomed in, and to his shock, Deptha realized he was looking at a swarm of drones, hundreds of them engaged in a battle at the top of the building.

"Are they still alive?" The desperation in his voice was now accentuated by panic at the sight of what he was looking at.

"Yes. However, their vitals are worsening," answered the computer.

Dep felt an overwhelming sense of dread taking over.

He needed a miracle.

4

Tanner looked up as the drone lowered level to his face.

He felt cold and numb as blood pooled beneath him.

The Visio appeared with the lurid face of V, her smile, her decrepit visage, staring at him, gloating over the moment.

"I guess you're happy now?" he managed to utter as the pain escalated and the blood continued to drain from him.

She grinned. "You brought this on yourself, Tanner. No one else is to blame. I gave you the opportunity to take the smart way, you chose this."

"The smart way?" he coughed as a spittle of blood erupted from his lips. "There is no right way with you, V, there is just your way, and I'd rather die than live in your fucking utopia."

"So be it," she said. "Good-bye, Tanner McNeal."

The Visio faded as the drone moved back – preparing to fire.

5

Dep studied the spectral scan in front of him, one that clearly showed exactly where his crew mates were located on that upper floor.

His mind raced for an answer.

There must be a way to stop them, he thought.

The *Dauntless* was not a military craft, he knew that. It had no weapons and no defense system, nothing he could directly use against the drones, but even as that thought faded into the miasma of hectic and desperate confusion, the idea suddenly came to him – like a bolt from the sky.

"Computer, is the EMP intact?"

"Affirmative."

"How long will it take to charge?"

"Thirty-three seconds."

"Do it! Activate it as soon as it reaches capacity."

Suddenly, as if on cue, as if they realized the threat hovering nearby, a sizable portion of the swarm turned and surged at the *Dauntless*, unleashing a hail of pellets.

The drones threw themselves at the *Dauntless*, like Kamikaze pilots, in a vain attempt to break through its crust.

The brutal pounding against the hull of the ship was terrifying, a maddening thunder of machines smashing themselves to pieces in a mad attempt, no doubt at the command of Lady V, to damage the ship.

Despite the horrendous concussion, Dep knew the Dauntless would hold up. It had withstood sixteen years in space, and not only the reentry to Earth's atmosphere, but the occasional pounding of space debris and rocks, pounding and denting, but never violating the integrity of its hull.

Just then the computer announced, "EMP activated!" and in an instant, the world changed.

Like a tornado suddenly stopped in its tracks, the drones stood motionless, as if paralyzed by an unseen force.

Hundreds of them just hung there, like the momentary pause in a grand choreography – and then, they dropped, like rocks falling from the sky, smashing into the ground far below - creating a virtual graveyard of Ai.

"Land the ship, now" commanded Dep as he dashed for the exit.

6

The 25th floor of Tetra-Drone was as silent as a moratorium.

Not a word was uttered. No one moved.

The state of shock and sheer consternation that riveted everyone, who had just witnessed the brutal and unforgivable attack on their own kind, had not only immobilized every soul in that room – it had shifted the very paradigm.

The New America, under Lady V, was no longer the paradise they believed it to be. The New America now had shades of the past, the very culture they had fought to leave behind, had now seeped into the veins of the nation – and at the hands of its leader, revealed the depth of her insanity.

Lady V stood there like a statuesque carved in marble – her eyes locked on the carnage she had just created within the Center, the nation's capital, and on the streets of Atlanta.

In her mind, she had just subdued an insurrection, a revolt and civil war against law and order and the very governance of the nation – *her* nation.

For her it was just another victory.

She turned, looking into the faces of those staring back at her, and for the first time V saw something in their faces she had not seen before; like bitter-sweet confusion, mixed with a growing and collective demeanor that resonated not adoration, but resentment; not love, but an undercurrent of rage and hatred.

No longer were they looking at her with awe or reverence, instead, their faces mirrored something else – repulsion, sheer utter repugnance.

Every woman in that room was, at that very instant, a mirror reflection of millions more across New America, and the world, those who had witnessed in bitter shock, as the drones descended on the crowd in Atlanta, unleashing a deadly storm of pellets which killed countless hundreds in just seconds. It was a massacre, a horrid and shocking and overwhelming sight, as the bloodied bodies lay twisted and heaped on the ground, and as the cries of both the injured and the survivors echoed around the world.

V crimped her jaws with an authoritative stance and turned to her most trusted of the Women's Guard.

"Take me to the helicopter, now" she commanded.

The four guards formed a flank on her left and right, and as they did, employees stepped in front of them, blocking their passage, their angry eyes fixed on her. "You're not going anywhere," one of them announced.

V sneered. "Move or you will be shot."

The women did not budge, in fact, more women piled in. "You'll have to shoot us all."

Already gripped by paranoia, V's rage exploded.

"Shoot her," she pointed to the lead woman.

Two of the guards leveled their weapons at her, but before they could trigger them, a loud concussion rang out and their chests erupted in a splatter of bright crimson as both guards dropped to the floor, dead.

V stood shocked as a group of WG's approached, their helmets removed, and their eyes and weapons locked on her and the remaining two guards.

"Lady V, you are under arrest for the murder of innocent civilians. Resist, and we will be forced to shoot," they aimed their weapons.

"You have no authority, you are under my command," she asserted with an arrogant step forward. One of the two guards pressed her weapon firmly against the President's chest.

"We don't answer to you anymore, we answer to the Resistance. Now, move your fucking ass before I put a bullet in you!"

7

Tanner opened his eyes as a ripple of pain cascaded over his entire body.

With a sigh of relief, he suddenly realized he was alive; moreover, that he was lying in the sickbay, aboard the *Dauntless*.

It was a secure feeling, as if the *Dauntless* was the only true home he had left in this world.

The last thing he remembered before blacking-out, was the face of Lady V and then the drone readying for the kill – and then nothing.

A slight rustle caught his attention.

He turned to see Mav, lying in the adjacent bunk, his eyes fluttering briefly and then they opened, as if on cue. Mav turned to face him with his immutable smirk.

"Hey there sunshine," he said with a grimace.

"You look like shit," said Mav.

"You don't look so good yourself."

Mav tried to move but the pain was too much. "Fuck, that hurts."

"It should," sounded a voice as Dep stepped into the sickbay. "How are you two feeling?" he asked, a smile forming on his lips.

"Like a truck landed on me," answered Mav.

The Indian's head bobbled agreeably.

Mav finally forced himself to a sitting position, taking a deep breath to squelch the pain and then fixed his eyes on Dep. "How'd you do it, was it the EMP?"

Dep nodded.

"Smart. Very smart."

"I didn't plan it that way," started Dep, "but when I saw the swarm it occurred to me that the quantum drives created an immensely powerful electro-magnetic pulse which could nullify anything electronic within five hundred meters of the ship. It was just a matter of letting it build up in the ship's capacitor and then unleashing it."

Mav tapped the hull of the ship, with tender regard. "She still has a few tricks up her sleeve."

"Indeed, she does," answered Dep with admiration in his voice.

"What happened to the others," asked Tanner, his concern now reflected in his face.

Dep became solemn and he hesitated a moment before answering.

"Brenner and Petar are pretty beat up, but they should pull through. They are in the next bay over, plus two more men we found down in the lobby who had survived."

"What about Matis and Cal?" asked Tanner with a hesitant tone, as if he already knew the answer.

"They didn't make it, Cap."

-VII-

1

Tel lurched up from the bed as a throaty gasp emitted from her lips.

Sweat covered her entire body, like a blanket of early-morning dew.

Her breaths came in short gulps.

The nightmares had become the norm – visiting its haunting visions upon her and releasing the encysted bubble of emotion and pain she had tried so hard to lock away.

Like so many countless millions across the nation, and the world, she had witnessed, in stark horror, as the drones slaughtered hundreds of women that day in Atlanta.

Moreover, she remembered the demeanor on Lady V's face, the look of sickening vengeance that played in her eyes, as if those innocent women were paying the price for assaulting her sense of entitlement and authority.

Hardly a day, and certainly not a single night, had passed since the tragedy, without being visited by the specter.

She understood what it must have felt like, when nuclear weapons vaporized millions in South and then North Korea; and the utter depth of morose apathy that must have consumed everyone when the asteroids struck.

With a gentle sigh of relief, as her reality replaced the ghoulish images, her eyes idly roamed the semi-darkness of the hotel room, slowly adjusting to the warm slivers of light which filtered through the curtains, waiting as her breathing calmed and as the ghosts of her nighttime visitation began to fade back into the dark recesses of her mind.

Hopefully, time will heal the pain, she thought, but in truth, she knew that it was a hard pain, a terrible one, imprinted on her very soul, and one she could hardly ever forget.

Her eyes finally settled on Tanner, next to her. A smile crept to her lips as she gently touched a forefinger to his shoulder, tracing the pockmarked surface of his skin, the raw vestiges of pellets which had cut into him – nearly taking him away from her, but certainly leaving their marks forever.

With a graceful twist, she swung her legs from the bed and strolled to the window and pulled the curtains apart to let the sunlight flood in.

The sun, in all its glory, smiled at her, presenting, as always, its wonderful cornucopia of life-giving energy to arouse her senses.

Tanner cracked an eye, rolled over and seeing her standing there in the flood of light, entirely naked, suddenly stirred him.

"Did I wake you?" she asked as she turned – exposing all of her femininity.

"Nah, was just lying here thinking about a good cup of coffee, but now…" he paused with a slight leer in his eye, "I'm suddenly thinking about something else."

Tel moved with cat-like stealth, slipped onto the bed, and straddled his body, her silver-white hair cascading down over her shoulders as she pressed herself into him and then whispered, "Coffee can wait."

2

The air was filled with a somber tranquility as thousands crowded onto the grounds surrounding the Lincoln Memorial, overlooking the Potomac River.

To one side of the Memorial stood the Center, Lady V's remaining legacy. The building was entirely empty. No one wanted any part of it. In fact, it was already scheduled for demolition.

Each person present held a white candle in their hands – a sea of flickering flames which lit up the twilight of encroaching nightfall.

Mother Nature, as if in veneration for the fallen, had quieted her winds, offering solace and calm to the ceremony.

Nancy Monroe, formerly known as Z, and leader of the Resistance, now acting as interim President of the nation, stood at the base of the broad steps leading up to the memorial.

She faced the throng with a single candle of her own. Its flame accentuated her wrinkled visage and betrayed the deep sorrow in her eyes.

To one side of where she stood, were rows of small white flags which stretched to the very edge of the Potomac itself, each one of them representing those who had lost their lives in the battle to achieve this moment in time.

When she spoke, her voice could be heard like the gentle touch of summer rain.

"Today we honor our fallen sisters and brothers, those who fought bravely for this moment in history. We honor their names and their sacrifice, and we honor their timeless souls. Please join me in a moment of silent remembrance."

When the eulogy was done, she stepped over to an object standing three meters in height, draped in dark cloth. Without a word, she pulled the draping and let it fall to the ground, revealing a monolithic black slab, and inscribed on its face were these words:

Equality is not a privilege,
– it is a right.
Dedicated to those who sacrificed everything to protect that right.

3

The small windowless room, an austere space, was adorned by just one square fold-up table and two chairs in its center.

Edna Bright sat on one side.

She was no longer accorded the honor of being addressed as Lady V, and certainly not the President.

Today, she was a prisoner in two worlds; the world without and the world within, and doubtless it was that the more powerful of the two was the storm that raged inside of her.

Her arrogant defiance, the swagger, the bearing of unchallengeable authority, all of it was gone, replaced by an unforgiving depth of moroseness, a dark cloud of despondency fixed to her face like angry black strokes on a painter's canvas.

There was no glamor, no strutting, no posing in the spotlight – just a lonely sad figure, the shadow of what she had been, even, the shadow of who she really was.

As she stared at the table, her mind no longer heard the voice of her mentor – that voice she had listened to all those years, one that told her everything she was doing was right and justifiable. A voice that compelled her – but not the voice reason.

Now, all she could hear was the maddening echo of taciturnity, a depthless vortex of nothing which replaced her ambitions, her dreams, and her sense of endless power.

The door opened as a guard stepped in.

Edna Bright stole a tentative glance, snickering as her lips formed into a sneer as Nancy Monroe entered the room.

"Come to rub my face in it some more?" she said without looking up.

Nancy sat across from her, looking at her with eyes that could easily have been mirrors of hate or repulsion, but instead, they pulsed with empathy.

She spoke, her voice firm and yet soft.

"No, Edna, I am not here to make you feel guilty. I am here to tell you that our decision is to release you."

Edna looked up at the elderly woman - her face rank with confusion. "I don't understand."

"We are not reinstituting prisons. Those days are gone. Criminals, like yourself, will have to face society on its terms, by working and contributing to it and paying your debt to society by contributing to it, not by wasting tax-payer dollars locked inside prison walls and guarded like a rabid dog."

She paused to look her straight in the eyes. "Of course, certain sanctions will be imposed. You will have to wear an ankle bracelet for some years so that we can keep track of your whereabouts. You will have to work and earn your own keep. There will be no handouts. But, if you start contributing to society, you can eventually earn back your complete freedom."

She lingered, watching the suspicious and incredulous eyes that looked back at her.

"Your fate is to face those you harmed."

Edna's head rocked back and forth, her eyes reflecting a new storm of emotions suddenly roiling within.

"No one will help me out there. That is a prison sentence of its own," her words hushed from her lips as she lowered her eyes to the table, like a truculent child.

Nancy smiled. "That is entirely up to you, Edna. She lingered for a moment, "I remember the day when Edna Bright inspired us at a time when the sky had been darkened by the falling asteroids, and the world felt as if it might end. I remember an Edna Bright who showed us a different side, someone who cared, someone who tried to put a fractured world back together again." She paused. "Is any shred of that Edna Bright still there?"

After a long silence, she answered, barely audible. "I don't know."

"I hope, for your sake, that you can find that part of you again, because you are going to face hell out there. You are hated and reviled by the very people who once adored you. If you have any chance of ever redeeming yourself, you will have to convince them that you are redeemable, and that Edna Bright, the good side of you, is back."

The President stood and turned to leave the room, but Edna spoke, her voice cracking to a bare whisper.

"How can you possibly trust me after what I did?"

The President turned to her. "Because I believe the human soul is capable of fixing whatever shit it gets itself into, Edna – even monsters like Lady V."

-VIII-

Months later…

In the wake of the *Reformation*, the name given for the period that followed, a Summit of nations was convened in Brussels. Its first order of business was the redaction of *The Inhumane Act.*

In the end, every provision remained intact, except one; men were now restored to equal status in society. The laws defining equality were clearly and strictly worded, mandating that no man, under any circumstances, could ever abuse a woman, physically, mentally, or sexually, and that no man, by whatever means, ideology or religion, could subjugate a woman's rights as a human being. The provision, although restoring men's equivalency, was clearly worded in such a way that if any man attempted to discriminate against a woman because of her gender, back-seat her, or deny her equal opportunity, that all hell would rain down on them. The law also applied in reverse, that is, with equal regard for infractions committed by women against men.

The redacted version was met with enthusiasm, in fact, surprisingly, even in countries where ideology and religious beliefs had previously marginalized women for centuries.

The chairperson for the League of Islamic Nations summed it up best in her speech at the Summit, which was heard the world over.

"As chairperson of the League of Islamic Nations, we affirm our commitment to upholding the Inhumane Act, the most significant manifesto ever created on behalf of the unified nations of the world and all humanity. We also affirm our commitment to the new age of women in the Islamic world – a world where women are free to be, to do and to have whatever freedoms they want. We affirm our respect and love for our God – and in turn, we believe that our God respects us and sees this transition as a natural progression in our growth. Religion, of whatever faith, should provide hope of finding something greater in ourselves. It should never be a prison that fetters the soul with arbitrary dictates and unchallengeable ideology. God be with you.

Epilogue

Many months had passed, time spent not only healing their wounds, but reacclimating to the new world, a rapidly changing one.

Tanner and Tel had finally accomplished the impossible; that is, if travelling to Jupiter and back, and then overcoming V's regime was not enough; they had finally gotten married and hitched their wagons to the same star.

Upon return from their protracted honeymoon, Tanner discovered that the President had appointed him the Director of NASA.

Her mandates included putting NASA back on the map again; with its first priority being designing and launching an early-warning system that would permanently reside in the asteroid belt between Mars and Saturn which would provide a constant vigil and defensive line against lethal rocks ever coming Earth's way; and finally, and no less important, to discover the source of *Footprint*, evidence of another race of beings who had visited Europa.

Within weeks, Tanner and the team were set up at the Johnson Space Center in Houston, which had sat idle and forgotten for nineteen years.

They cleared out the cobwebs, got people in to clean it up and give it a fresh look, and began hiring outside-the-box thinkers who wanted to be part of the advanced curve on space exploration.

One day, as the team sat in the cafeteria, chattering over coffee, Dep stumbled into the room, gasping for breath.

He had just sprinted the full gamut of the complex from the building where he worked, over half a kilometer away. Why he did not use a phone, nobody knew, but then again, that was Dep – brilliant, resourceful, but sometimes a bit too conventional.

"You have to see this," he announced as the sweat dribbled down the sides of his face.

No one stopped to ask, they just followed the small Indian as he turned and disappeared from the room.

When they caught up with him, Dep was already hanging over a countertop which housed multiple computer screens, his eyes practically popping from their sockets.

"You've got our attention," said Tanner, "what's up, Dep?"

He touched a finger to one screen and pointed to a schematic showing bars in a repeating pattern.

"Those amplitudes," he turned to look at them, "…were not there an hour ago."

Tanner leaned closer, his eyes poring over the screen. "Okay, what's the point?"

Dep nodded to the adjacent computer. "That is what those readings looked like earlier today. See, they are mostly flatlined with occasional minor erratic fluctuations – nothing significant. It is what we usually see when we study *space noise*. But this," he jabbed a finger at the other screen, "these amplitudes are massive and they're consistent – repeating every thirty seconds on the dot."

Tel raised a brow. "Are you saying this is not space clatter?"

Dep nodded. "That's exactly what I'm saying." He turned to face the group. "Remember?! Before leaving Europa, we set up micro-dishes aimed into the sky beyond Jupiter, in the hopes of picking up any echoes from beyond the rim of the giant. Maybe even getting a glimpse of whoever left those traces of *Footprint*? These amplitudes," he pointed again, "were picked up by those very dishes."

Tanner's brows twisted close together. "Are you saying what I think you're saying?" he asked. Dep tapped another computer, the air of excitement about him was now contagious. "I ran the input through **CET**…"

"Remind me again, what is **CET**?" asked Mav.

Camilla spoke up, "He's referring to **C**ontact-**ET**, a computer program designed over two decades ago by **JPL** to separate out chatter coming from black holes, nebula, and other star clusters, essentially, to identify patterns which might indicate intelligent life."

"Actually," added Dep excitedly, "**CET** is an offshoot of a program developed by the **SETI** team...

"Okay, we get it Dep," said Tanner with a wave of his hand, "… please get to the point."

His head bobbed excitedly side to side.

"It's a message, guys. I have checked it a dozen times. **CET** arrives at the same interpretation every time. You see, it is not a different language, it is a phonetic syllabic, a mimic of our own language."

"Meaning?" probed Tanner, his patience now at the edge.

Dep tapped the screen and one word popped up.

"This is what **CET** has deciphered from that frequency."

They stared incredulously at a single word on the screen.

HELLO

Dep smiled, "Someone is trying to contact us, guys."

He lingered a moment, his smile widening.

"Here's the real killer," he said as he tapped the computer once again, revealing a map of the stars. "I can tell you exactly where that signal is coming from."

For more books by Réal Laplaine visit his website at
www.reallaplaine.com

Réal Laplaine

Author

www.ingramcontent.com/pod-product-compliance
Lightning Source LLC
LaVergne TN
LVHW050532160826
845677LV00011B/2012

* 9 7 9 8 2 3 0 4 2 2 5 4 9 *